The Mailbox

Introducing Elizabeth Stitchway, P

MARY JANE FORBES

Todd Book Publications

The Mailbox

ISBN: 9780615943947 (sc)

Printed in the United States of America
Todd Book Publications: 05/2010
Third Release: 9/2017
Port Orange, Florida

Author photo: Ami Ringeisen
Cover design: Mary Jane Forbes
Cover re-design: 9/2017

The Mailbox

Chapter 1

——

THE ENGINEER BLASTED THE train's whistle warning pedestrians and all vehicles to stay clear of the crossing as the train sped through the last intersection before the river.

"Slow down. Slow down," the man yelled crawling out of the boxcar as he tried to maintain his footing. His pleas were lost in the noise of the train's wheels grinding over the tracks. He stretched his left hand and arm out as far as possible, but he couldn't quite reach the ladder. He tried again. His fingers kept slipping off the cold metal bar. Holding his breath, stretching a third time, straining every muscle in his arm, he gripped the steel ladder attached to the side of the rusty-red CSX freight container.

He clutched the ladder's rung, leaned away from the boxcar as far as he dared trying to catch a glimpse of the water he knew was ahead. He could see the trestle spanning the river. Pulling himself back flat to the ladder he scrambled to the top. A protruding piece of metal caught his brown canvas backpack. He yanked it free. The strength of the hot, humid wind from the movement of the train hurtling forward plastered his black slacks and windbreaker against his body, swept his thick sandy-brown hair away from his pasty face. The train bore down on the approaching trestle.

The man yelled again. "Why aren't you stopping? You always stop here. Stop!"

The boxcar passed over the bank of the river, its water flowing under the trestle. The man still clinging to the slimy top rung of the ladder looked down at the fast running water. The thirty-first car in line behind the engine rolled toward the middle of the river. Another thirty seconds and the boxcar would once again be traveling over land.

"Now! Now," he shouted, urging himself to make the leap.

With all of his might, the man jumped praying he would clear the steel beams and cement bed of the train trestle and land in the water. With eyes closed, he felt the wind take hold of his body, pushing him away from the boxcar. Seconds later the rushing water dragged his body under.

Fighting the current, the man surfaced and began to swim. He could see the weather-beaten dock ahead, the dock he knew so well. It wasn't far. He kept up his battle against the rushing water— sometimes winning, sometimes not.

It was mid-afternoon, the sun forcing the ninety-five-degree temperature higher and higher. A typical summer day in Florida but the weather was changing, and the tide was in full retreat. He could see ominous clouds in the distance as he continued his fight against the current.

Each time he came up for air he saw the storm advancing from the west—angry black clouds closing in. He heard nothing but the splashing of his arms, his choking on water that managed to enter his windpipe as he gasped for each breath.

Approaching the water-soaked dock, he struggled to gain his footing. The current dragged him under one last time before he felt the muddy river bank underfoot. He slowly hauled his body and backpack up the short, debris-laden boat ramp bordered by the dock. Clear of the water he rolled onto his back gasping for air, air thick with the musty scent of vegetation and mildew. A squirrel jumped onto the trunk of a nearby oak tree, stopped to look at the body on the ground beneath him, and then scampered up the tree instinctively seeking shelter from the approaching storm.

Lying on the ground, the man's breathing slowly began returning to normal. A smile formed on his lips. He was back. He could now put his plan into action. A plan he had developed over the last year and a half in prison—a plan to extract his revenge.

Chapter 2

——

"ONLY TWENTY MORE MAILBOXES. Come on, Elizabeth, you can make it." She slapped the steering wheel of her mail truck. She was sure she could finish her route before the hurricane ripped through Turtle Grove Estates. The sun was still shining in the east, but the west wind was building, the black clouds closing fast as she scooted from mailbox to mailbox. She jammed the mail, circulars, and small packages into their gaping mouths then gunned her vehicle to the next stop.

Elizabeth twisted the knob of her weather radio. "Let's see what you guys are predicting now."

The radio crackled to life. "...and anyone in Flagler, Volusia, or Brevard counties take shelter immediately. Hurricane Dora has been upgraded to a category three in the last half hour. It's beating down on Orlando and approaching the east coast, north and south, of Daytona Beach at ninety-six miles per hour."

"Orlando. I have twenty-five minutes." Elizabeth's cell phone pierced her jangled nerves. She dug around in her pansy-painted tote never stopping her forward motion. She held the phone to her ear.

"Elizabeth, are you there?"

"Yes, Mr. Perkins."

"Get yourself back to the post office. The hurricane switched direction. Port Orange is in its direct path. Do you hear me?"

"Yes, sir. I'm on my way."

Elizabeth kept the pressure on the gas pedal. She approached a stretch of trees marching along the backside of a canal designed to handle the downpours known to cause flooding in central Florida. The wind was getting stronger, whipping branches, hurling dead palm fronds against her vehicle.

"Come on, Elizabeth. Keep going, eyes on the road. Only a few more stops and then you can make a run for it."

The rain switched from large splashes to sheets of water, buckets of water thrown at her, one after the other. Her left turn onto Red Snapper Lane, the last row of houses was only a few yards ahead. The rushing canal water already near the top of its banks continued to rise as the torrential rain began to batter the land.

Suddenly a burst of gale-force wind caught the side of her red, white, and blue mail truck, lifting it up, carrying it sideways to the bank along the canal. The wheels on the right side caught the crest of the bank tripping the vehicle.

"Oh, my mail. No. No," Elizabeth cried out as the vehicle tumbled into the canal landing on its side half submerged in the rushing, murky water. She didn't feel her mouth hit the top of the steering wheel when the truck landed cutting her lip, or the gash on her knee from the bottom of the dashboard as the water surged into the truck.

"Stop. Stop!"

She grabbed pieces of mail as they floated by. Mail piled up against the windshield as she tried to stuff them into a white canvas bag now gray soaked with water. White bins from the rear of the truck floated to the front hitting Elizabeth in the neck. She was now up to her shoulders in water. A large plastic bin floating near the open window opposite the driver's side tumbled through the opening spilling the contents into the rushing stream.

"Hey, lady, are you alright?" a man yelled dropping his brown canvas backpack on the grass as he slid into the canal, sinking up to his chest in the fast current.

"No, I'm not alright," Elizabeth cried out. "My mail, it's floating away."

"Let me help you."

She couldn't make out what he said over the howling wind. The man struggled through the rushing water to get to Elizabeth as she escaped through the open window of the truck along with another bin. She lurched to retrieve a small package and slipped under the water. The man grabbed her around the waist and turned to battle back to the bank of the canal. Reaching out, arms flailing behind the man who had a vice-like grip around her, Elizabeth grabbed the rope of the canvas bag now half filled with mail for the remaining houses on her route. He pulled her tight against his body. She held fast to the bag.

Reaching the side of the canal, getting a toehold in the muck, he dragged Elizabeth and her bag over the top. They both lay on the grassy lip, gasping for breath their faces pelted with pinpricks of driving rain. Elizabeth's strawberry-red Capris and matching sneakers were smeared with mud as was her daisy-flowered T-shirt. Her yellow ball cap was long gone.

"Thanks, mister—" She stopped mid-sentence, letting out a piercing scream.

The man followed her horrified stare back to the truck. A body floated down the canal and was caught against the back end of the mail vehicle. An arm, dangling out of its wrapping, whipped one way and then another as debris bumped against it.

The man losing his footing slid back into the canal. The speed of the flowing river carried him to the body snared by the vehicle. With one arm wrapped around the torso, he again resumed his fight to the edge of the canal dragging the body with him. Elizabeth, on her knees, reached out and grabbed the arm dangling out of its wrapping. Together they pulled the dead weight out of the water, dragged it onto the grass. Exhausted, gulping for air, the man rolled over on the ground beside the body.

He looked over at Elizabeth, the canvas mailbag at her side as rain continued to pour over her hair and clothes. She fished her cell phone out of its water-tight case, punched in some numbers, and yelled into the receiver. The man caught bits and pieces as Elizabeth shouted directions to where she was. Hands shaking, she stuffed the phone back into the case and looked back at the man.

"Mister, are you okay?" she yelled over the howling wind.

"Yah. Who did you call?"

"911. Is the...is the person dead?"

"Very."

Hearing a siren, Elizabeth scooted down the small berm of the canal to the street, dragging the mailbag behind her. A squad car slowly rounded the bend in the road, red lights flashing. It pulled to a stop beside Elizabeth standing on the edge of the grass. Two officers jumped out of either side of the black and white vehicle, black raincoats whipping around them with each gust, and ran toward her stumbling as they tried to maintain their balance against the biting wind.

"Miss, are you alright?" one of the officers yelled.

"Yes, I think so, but my vehicle...over there in the ditch. I tried to stay on the road, but this wind...a big gust picked me up and...I landed on my side in the canal. Oh, my boss is going to be so upset...I tried to get the mail...but it started to float away—"

"Here, miss, let's get you in the car."

"My bag...my bag...don't forget my mailbag...here let me help."

"Miss, we've got the bag, now in the car you go. There's a slicker on the seat. Put it on."

"Wait, there's a body up there."

"A body? Where?"

"Up there on the grass. See." Elizabeth shook her finger pointing up to the edge of the canal. The man...he...where is he?"

"I see the body, miss. But, I don't see a man."

"He was here. He helped me. He went back and pulled the body up to the edge...he..."

An officer crawled up the grass to the large mound where Elizabeth was pointing. The other officer slid into the front seat of the car. Elizabeth, now in the back seat, pulled on the black slicker. Holding tight to the rope of the canvas bag on the floor next to her, she stared out the window at the officer dragging the wrapped corpse down the slick grassy slope.

"Dispatch. This is car 257. I've got the lady who called in about the accident in Turtle Grove Estates. Seems we have a body. It's brutal out here. I'll put it in a body bag and transport it to the morgue. It's wrapped in something...looks like a blanket. No point sending the wagon out in this stuff."

Elizabeth retrieved her cell phone and punched the numbers for the post office. "Mr. Perkins, this is Elizabeth, Elizabeth Stitchway," she shouted over the wind. "I know you told me to return to the yard...yes, it's dangerous out. Oh, Mr. Perkins, my vehicle is on its side in a canal...I couldn't help it. What? I can't hear you...the wind. I'm in a police car...Yes, I'll wait for you."

"Miss, who are you talking to?"

"My boss, Mr. Perkins. He's the postmaster. He wants me to wait here. He's sending a tow truck."

"Miss, get back in the car. We're not leaving you here alone."

Chapter 3

———

FLASHING YELLOW LIGHTS PIERCED the sheets of rain as the tow truck pulled to a stop facing the squad car. The truck's high beams hit the two officers and Elizabeth in the eyes through the windshield. A man in a yellow slicker jumped out of the truck. Head bent into the rain, he rushed to the squad car as an officer struggled to push the door open against the wind. Keeping up the pressure on the door, he slid out of the car, the door slipping through his fingers slammed shut. A gust hit the officer full force pinning him to the closed door.

"Elizabeth, Elizabeth Stitchway. Where is she?" the man asked, *T. Perkins* stamped on the left side of his yellow slicker. The truck driver hunched next to him in a black rain-drenched jumpsuit, Al embroidered on the pocket.

The officer pointed to the inside of the squad car, but Elizabeth was already out. Leaning into the wind, she called to her boss.

"Mr. Perkins, here...here I am."

"Where's your vehicle?"

"Up there," Elizabeth yelled pointing in the direction of the canal.

"Okay. Come on, Al. Let's see what we're up against," Perkins shouted.

Perkins and the truck driver scrambled up the slope to the ridge of the canal. Taking in the mail vehicle's situation, Al gave Perkins a thumbs up and headed back to his rig. Settling inside his truck, Al slowly swung around, backed up the slight rise to the canal, engaged the brakes, and jumped out leaving the truck running. He motioned to Perkins for help pulling the grappling hooks and chains from the iron rails of the tow truck. With hooks in hand, the two men slid down the canal's bank into the water. Fighting their way to the mail vehicle, they attached the hooks to the rear undercarriage on both sides. Returning to the truck, Al slowly raised the rear of the mail vehicle freeing it from the rushing muddy water like a child's toy dangling at the end of the chains. Al's foot increased the pressure on the gas pedal, the engine grinding as it inched forward.

Elizabeth and the two officers fought their way to the top of the berm. Watching the mail truck respond to the pressure of the hooks, they waved frantically to Al to keep going. As the mail truck crested the top of the bank, the tow truck gathered a speed so the smaller vehicle wouldn't rear-end him. Al slowed to a stop once both trucks were on the street.

Mr. Perkins, battling against the wind to stay on his feet, made his way back to Elizabeth and the two policemen. "Officer, can you take Miss Stitchway home?" he yelled.

"You bet. That was a nice rescue you guys performed."

"Thanks, Officer. I have to take good care of my babies. Let me know if there's anything else you need from me," Perkins said turning away from the rain beating on his face.

"We have to interview Miss Stitchway," the officer said. "Can she stop at the department tomorrow morning?"

"I'll certainly see that she's given time to meet you. Elizabeth, can you talk to the officer tomorrow before work?"

"Sure...sure. Is 7:30 okay with you, Officer, Officer...what's your name?"

"Detective Armstrong. Just ask for Detective Dick Armstrong. 7:30 will be fine. Now, let's get going. Drive carefully," Armstrong said to Al. "The power's out. Downed lines everywhere. Miss Stitchway, we'll drive you home. You'd better take care of that lip right away."

Elizabeth climbed into the squad car. Sitting inside she touched her lower lip, pulled back from a stab of pain wiping a bloody finger on her shirt.

Perkins knocked on the window and shouted, "Elizabeth, I'll see you in the morning after your interview with the officer. Stop in my office before you start sorting your mail."

Elizabeth nodded, pulling the black slicker around her body. She suddenly felt cold, wanting to go home to a hot shower.

"Tell me if you see the man, Miss Stitchway," Detective Armstrong said, looking in the rearview mirror at Elizabeth.

"The man?"

"The man you said helped you in the canal."

Chapter 4

—

PUSHING THE CEMENT RABBIT OFF its base, the man stooped down and picked up the brass key. He returned the rabbit to the center of the granite rock to continue its vigil of the backyard. Inserting the key into the lock, turning it to the right, he heard a click. The door gave way to the pressure of his shoulder. He was in.

"Walter, you really should have changed your locks," Joe muttered to himself.

The back door of the cream-stucco house opened into a large sunroom. He closed the door behind him and didn't move. Puddles formed around his feet as his eyes, adjusting to the dark due to the storm, darted from side to side. He had dreamed of this moment. He sat in the nearest chair, dropped his backpack to the floor, and pulled off his soggy shoe. Somewhere he had lost its mate. He continued to remove his clothes letting them pile up on the cold, white-tiled floor.

Whirling red lights from the police cruiser, the steady beam of yellow from the tow truck across the street, provided him intermittent shocks of light across the room. Standing naked, he peered out the window in the back door and watched the woman get into the cruiser. The tow truck with the mail vehicle chained to the back pulled away from the edge of the grass, disappearing down the street. The squad car followed. The sunroom fell into darkness.

Exhausted from the events of the day, the first thing on the man's mind was a shower. A smile crossed his face. It didn't matter if it was hot or cold. Anything would be better than the prison shower. He made his way down the hall to the master bedroom, then to the bathroom. Stepping into the shower, he turned the water on full. Within seconds, hot water was beating down on his body washing any vestiges of scum from his life in prison down the drain.

"Joe, my boy, it doesn't matter if there's electricity or not. You know this house better than that eight-by-ten-foot cell you've been living in for the past year and a half."

He began to sing.

He sang *Old Man River* at the top of his lungs, sometimes laughing at the irony of the words—he swam a river, and he saved a woman in the rushing water of a canal.

"Hell, life is good!"

Drying off with a big fluffy towel, he went back into the bedroom. Walking straight to the dresser, he pulled out a pair of jockey briefs, then to the closet and a pair of shorts from a shelf on the right and took what felt like a golf shirt from a hanger. Dressing quickly, Joe retraced his steps to the kitchen. Opening a cupboard where he had kept the liquor, he was pleased Walt still used the shelf for that purpose. He picked up a bottle, took a sniff, and screwed the cap back on.

"Scotch, my friend. Surely we have a bottle of scotch."

After sniffing two more bottles, he found what he was looking for.

"Now a glass...no problem."

Retrieving a glass from the cupboard next to the liquor, he stuck a finger in it, pouring the scotch up to his second knuckle, screwed the cap back on the bottle. He once again headed to the master bedroom.

He passed the thermostat but didn't stop. The house was warm and humid—the temperature rising. Without electricity for the AC unit, the air would soon be very uncomfortable. Joe didn't care because anything would be better than the cold, dank air in his cellblock.

Lying on the bed, he reached behind his head plumping up two pillows, laid back, and took a sip of his drink.

"Ahhh. How nice. Here's to you, Walt. I hope you've enjoyed living in my house, the house you swindled me out of. Your days are numbered. Whoever said revenge is sweet sure knew what he was talking about."

Joe continued sipping his scotch, slowly acclimating himself to the sensation of freedom. Savoring the last drop of his drink warming his throat, he leaned forward setting his empty glass on the bedside table. The wind continued to howl outside, rain and debris striking the windows, but to Joe, who every night tried to sleep with men yelling, with the clanging of steel as cell doors banged shut, the storm outside played like a lullaby. Tomorrow he would start executing his plan for revenge. Tonight...tonight he'd begin to rejuvenate his body.

Chapter 5

———

THE FRONT DOOR BURST OPEN. Martha Stitchway ran out to greet her daughter, wrapping her in a quilt. Elizabeth's father, Harry, waited in his wheelchair inside the entrance.

Detective Armstrong plopped the soaked mailbag at the front door. "Nasty night, folks. Take care of Elizabeth here. I'd say she's had a tough day at the office."

"We will, officer, and thanks for bringing her home," Martha said.

Ushered up the front steps, Elizabeth turned her head, waved at the police officers as they drove off in the pelting rain.

Stepping through the door into the comfort of her family, Elizabeth leaned over, kissed her father's cheek.

Folding the quilt tighter around his daughter, he stroked her damp red curls. "It's okay, sweetie. You're home safe now."

Martha closed the door against the storm and gave Elizabeth a quick hug.

"Mom, you can't believe how strong the wind blew."

"Lizzy, where's your truck?" Harry asked.

"Mr. Perkins had it towed."

The house was dark as was the street outside. The storm continued to block the early evening light. Harry pushed the wheel on his chair leading the way to the kitchen following the beam of his flashlight lying in his lap. Three candles burned cheerfully on the kitchen table, the air hot and humid. No electricity—no AC. Both of

Elizabeth's parents were dressed in light blue shorts topped with white T-shirts. Sweat stains crept around their waistbands.

"Harry, unwrap the peanut butter and jelly sandwiches, please, and oh yes, put out a bottle of water for Elizabeth. Come, dear, let's get you into some dry clothes and then your dad and I want to hear everything that happened."

Holding the quilt in place with both hands, Elizabeth looked around the kitchen. "Where's Maggie?"

"That dog of yours is under your bed and won't come out," Martha said. "When the wind started to howl something struck the side of the house. She darted into your room, and we haven't seen her since. Now off with those wet clothes before you catch your death."

"Mom, my shirt and Capris, they're plastered with dirt and look at my shoes. Can you get me something to put them in?" Elizabeth padded down the hall to her room with the aid of the flashlight. Martha followed with a laundry basket balancing two chubby red candles in the bottom.

"Mom, I need a bandage. Look, my knee...the cut isn't deep, but it could start bleeding again."

"Oh, my...and your lip. What shall we do about your lip?"

"A little ice?"

"Right. We still have some. I'll put out few cubes. The water is still pretty hot. I'm sure there's enough for a quick shower...and the stuff in your hair. Elizabeth, your hair looks like a rats nest. Fresh towels are on the rack. I put a candle on your bathroom sink. Come out to the kitchen when you're ready."

Struggling out of her drenched Capris, T-shirt, and underwear, Elizabeth put the dry clothes, her mother fished out of her dresser drawers, on the bed.

Standing in the shower, she let the hot water slosh over her skin. The flow of the water helped to settle her nerves a notch. She lathered up her hair and tried to pull a large tooth comb through the tangles. Stepping out of the shower she roughly rubbed herself dry. With the brisk rubbing and the warmth from the shower her shaking almost stopped but not completely. In the candlelight, she looked at the young woman in the bathroom mirror. The episodes of the past three hours seemed like a dream. But the cut on her lip and the scrape on her knee proved otherwise. They both throbbed.

She was pulled from her trance by Maggie's soft whining. Wrapped in her bathrobe, Elizabeth picked up the candle on the sink and returned to her bedroom. She put the flickering candle on the floor, laid down next to the bed, lifting the dust ruffle. A pair of eyes reflected the candle's flame. Maggie let out another whine but inched forward putting her paw on top of her mistress's hand.

"Come on girl. It's safe. Let's go eat."

The dog didn't budge.

"Now, really, Maggie, be a big brave dog and come on out."

Elizabeth stroked the dog's paw. Maggie inched forward, her nose now protruding from under the dust ruffle. The black and white Border Collie pressed flat to the floor didn't have much room to maneuver under the low bed.

"That's it. You can do it."

Maggie slithered out, kissed Elizabeth's hand and face knocking her over as she tried to sit up. Putting her arms around her dog, she laughed as she struggled to regain a sitting position. Elizabeth gave Maggie a good rub on her back, cooing how brave the dog was to come out of hiding.

Sitting on the floor, she leaned back against the bed. "Mags, I can't tell Mom and Dad how frightening the storm was. They have enough to worry about. I'll put a smile on my face...of course, Dad will see through my...my attempt to brush off how scary it was to be blown in the canal. That's okay, I'll tell him later. But Mom couldn't handle it, and that would upset Dad. So, Maggie, you and I are going to blow off the last few hours. As Dad, said, I'm home safe."

Feeling much better after the hot shower, Elizabeth blew out the candle on the floor, picked up the other candle on the dresser, gave a pat on Maggie's silky head, and joined her parents in the kitchen. A bottle of water and a sandwich on a red paper plate sat on the table in front of her chair.

Martha picked up a plate of cookies from the counter and repositioned the small battery-operated fan a little to the left. She paused a moment, smoothing a non-existent fly-away piece of brown hair streaked with silver, before putting the cookies on the table.

The wind buffeted their small manufactured home, and the sound of debris hitting the roof and aluminum siding could be heard over the latest bulletin from the weather radio. Maggie let out a yelp but didn't leave Elizabeth's side. The kitchen was cozy in the flickering candlelight—the lemon-yellow walls and cream-colored cabinets mellow in the shadows.

Harry sat at the head of the table in his wheelchair twisting a little to ease his back pain. He turned the radio down and leaned forward patting Elizabeth's hand. "You're safe now, pumpkin. Please, tell your mom and me what happened. All you said when you called is that there was an accident and the police were bringing you home."

"Dad, I will but first can I have a shot of your whiskey?"

"Oh, Elizabeth, do you think—"

Harry interrupted his wife. "Martha, she's thirty-one. If the girl wants a shot of whiskey, she gets a shot of whiskey. Now, please get Lizzy and me a glass while I get the bottle. Join us if you like." Harry rolled over the red brick patterned linoleum to the closet with the liquor, retrieved the bottle from the lower cabinet and returned to the table. He poured a healthy shot for his daughter and himself.

Elizabeth tapped her glass to her father's and to her mother's bottled water. Taking a sip, she closed her eyes and swallowed, letting the rich liquid warm her.

"That's nice. Thanks, Dad. How did it go at the rehab center this morning?"

"Pretty good. My therapist thinks I'll be able to start taking a few steps soon, but I'll have to wear some kind of a girdle to support my back."

"That's great news." Elizabeth leaned over to her father giving him a kiss on the cheek.

"Now, come on, Lizzy, enough about me. Tell us what happened."

"Well, I felt the storm picking up steam, and Mr. Perkins called telling me to head back. The wind gusts were gaining strength, and then the rain began. But, I really thought I had time to finish my route. My plan—"

"Honestly, Elizabeth, those plans of yours are going to get you into trouble yet," her mother said pushing the cookies to her daughter.

Maggie inched closer to Elizabeth's chair.

"As I was saying, my plan after finishing the deliveries was to drive home instead of to the post office yard. After all, you're only a couple of miles away. Which reminds me, Mom. Can you drive me to the post office tomorrow morning? My car's still there."

"Of course, dear."

"Anyway, I thought I could make it...from 8236 to 8246...that was it. Done! But all of a sudden this huge gust picked me up. I mean my vehicle. I could feel the wheels on my side hit the ground, and then my truck bounced into the runoff canal. Water was up around my shoulders instantly...and the mail started floating to the front piling up against the windshield. Fortunately, I had a mailbag with me, so I started to grab the pieces in front of me and to the side...but I couldn't keep up with it."

"Elizabeth, you should have saved your life first. You could have drowned," Martha said.

"But then, listen to this. The most amazing thing happened. I could hear a man's voice...calling to me."

"A man?"

"Yes, Mom. I didn't know where the voice was coming from, then he suddenly appeared in the water next to me. I had pulled myself out of my truck through the window. I was holding on to a mailbag and saw a package. I lunged for it and went under the water. The man must have been powerful because he pulled me up, made it to the bank, and somehow pushed me out of the canal. You wouldn't believe how fast the water was flowing."

"Thank, God, for this man," Harry said. "Is that when you called the police. I mean, how did they know to come to help you?"

"Wait. Wait. That was when I saw a body floating down the canal."

"A body? Oh, dear." Martha patted her hair down again.

"It was wrapped in something, maybe a blanket, and hit the back of my truck. It stopped...wedged against the bank and my truck, I guess."

"Then what?" Martha asked, taking a sip from her husband's drink, pushing the plate of cookies closer to him.

"The man slid back into the water and pulled the body to the bank, same as me."

"What made you think it was a body and not a big bag of trash?" Harry asked.

"Oh, Dad, an arm was sticking out, dangling back, straight out in the current. That's when I called 911 on my cell. Thanks again, Mom, for that waterproof case. It was a lifesaver today."

"Take a bite of your sandwich, dear, and try one of those cookies. Harry, let her catch her breath."

Elizabeth picked up her sandwich, but then abruptly looked back into her father's eyes. "Dad, the man disappeared."

"What do you mean he disappeared?"

"The squad car drove up, red lights whirling...honest, Dad, it was just like the movies." Elizabeth's eyes opened wide in amazement, her lips spreading in a smile, a little smile...because her lip hurt. She put an ice cube on the cut as she absentmindedly patted Maggie on the head, slipping her a piece of cookie while her mother went to the cupboard to replenish the plate.

"And?" Harry asked leaning forward to add a small splash of whiskey to Elizabeth's glass.

"Just that...he was gone. The officers climbed out of their squad car and were practically blown in my direction. I motioned to the body on the grass where the man pushed it and turned to say that man helped me, but I was pointing at thin air. He was nowhere in sight. Poof!"

Chapter 6

——

POSTMASTER TERRY PERKINS heard the soaked mailbag dragging on the floor before Elizabeth entered his office. He looked up to find her standing in front of his desk. Yesterday he saw Elizabeth at the canal covered with a black slicker, her drenched hair plastered to her face or whipped out straight by the wind. Today she was back to her colorful self—neon orange Capris, white T-shirt decorated with a profusion of poppies, lime green ball cap and matching sneakers. The only drab item near her was the water-logged mailbag now resting on the cement floor in front of his desk.

"How did it go at the police station?" Perkins asked.

"It was nothing really. I told Detective Armstrong the same thing I told him yesterday when he drove me home."

"I see. Well, your truck isn't back from the repair shop yet. They did call. There wasn't any damage, but it'll take a couple of days to swab out the mud. The mechanic reported that it's bad inside. The grassy slope evidently cushioned the fall, but they still want to be sure the brakes are working and give it a wash job. Can't have you running around in a muddy U.S. postal vehicle."

"No, sir. We can't have that."

"Here are the keys to 923. Drive it today. Hopefully, yours will be back before the weekend. You better go now—get your mail sorted. You're getting a late start so you'll have to hurry."

"Yes, sir. I will, sir. What should I do with this mail? It's still wet."

"Sort what you can...include it in today's run. Throw out the flyers. Once your bin is loaded, lay the really wet stuff on your sorting table. Maybe it will dry out enough so you can deliver it tomorrow."

"Yes, sir."

Elizabeth let out a sigh as she headed to the sorting room. She wasn't sure what to expect from her boss after she landed her truck in the canal. Now she knew. *Geez,* she thought, *Mr. Perkins wasn't very nice. He didn't even ask about my cut lip.* "Hi, Helen."

"Tough luck yesterday, Lizzy," Helen called out.

The sorting area was stifling. Even on the best of days, the air conditioner had a hard time keeping up with the summer heat. The electricity had been restored sometime during the night, but the air still had the oppressive feel of humidity from the hurricane's torrential rainfall.

All the carriers were hustling, sorting their mail, piling the stacks into the large orange rolling bins. They looked like coal cars in a mine, but instead of black lumps, these carts were piled high with colorful sheets of paper, white envelopes, and small packages wrapped in brown paper. One by one the crew pushed their bins through the swinging doors and on out to the mail truck yard—soldiers waiting to go into another day's battle. Each carrier transferred their bundles from the orange bins into their vehicles in an order only they could decipher. Without looking up, they shouted comments to one another about yesterday's storm—did their co-worker get home before the hurricane hit, and if not where were they when they were caught? "Lucky you," was called out to those with short runs allowing them to beat the advancing angry clouds before the wind and rain set in.

I would have to have one of the biggest routes, Elizabeth thought. It seems most everyone missed the fun but me.

After her dad was injured in a work-related accident, Elizabeth moved back home to help out. She took the first job she could get close to home with regular hours. Working part-time at the post office, she finally got her own route stepping into the shoes of a retiree. Fortunately, it was a light mail day—not many flyers, no magazines, and no end-of-the-month bills. But Elizabeth's bin was still filled to the brim. She had to be careful as she pushed through the swinging doors to number 923. Quickly packing her truck, she slipped inside, started the engine, and headed out of the yard. Her plan to stop at her house to pick up Maggie had not changed. A little apprehensive about what she might find the day after the violent storm, what with her being blown into the canal and, God Almighty, the body, she needed her furry friend. It was against postal rules to have a dog in the truck with her. She rarely went against the rules but today was one of those days.

Elizabeth pulled into her parent's driveway and for the first time took note of the storm's damage to their manufactured home. Hearing the vehicle, Maggie stood waiting at the door, tail wagging in anticipation of greeting her mistress. Elizabeth threw a quick kiss to her dad as he handed her the leash restraining the prancing dog. She opened the back end of the little truck, and Maggie jumped in.

Standing in the driveway, Elizabeth called to her father. "Dad, did you know a section of the carport is torn off?"

"That's what your mother said. I called the maintenance office, and they're sending someone over. You be careful driving. It's all over the news warning that power lines are down, but they reported most of the stop lights are working."

Driving out of her parent's development, Elizabeth made a bee-line for the beginning of her route, two miles down the road. Looking in the rearview mirror, she gave Maggie her instructions.

"You know you have to lay down, and no barking. No matter what you hear…no barking."

Maggie scrunched forward on her belly answering with a soft whine.

"Honestly, Maggie, you wouldn't believe how scary it was yesterday. And now look at today. The sun is bright, not a cloud in the sky, not even a breeze. But the air is sure heavy after all that rain."

The streets were littered with huge palm fronds, branches of all sizes, and a few lawn chairs that the owners had left outside and were blown into a neighbor's yard. Elizabeth kept her eyes peeled on the road for fear she'd hit something. "That's all I'd need...hit a branch, dent good old 923. Perkins would fire me for sure."

Elizabeth methodically stopped at each house receiving mail, opened the mailbox door, stuffed in the mail, flipped the door up, and went on to the next. The red flag was up on some alerting Elizabeth that there was something in the box waiting to be picked up.

She approached the grassy strip bordering the canal. "Maggie, you and I are going to get out and take a look. When confronted with a place where something bad happened, it's best to go back and look it in the face Dad says. So, Maggie, that's what we're going to do."

She slowly pulled to a stop on the edge of the grass and turned off the engine. Birds were chirping, and several squirrels darted up a nearby tree. Getting out of the truck, she walked around to the back and let Maggie jump down. Maggie saw a squirrel, her ears shot up, and she let out a soft bark looking back and forth from her mistress to the squirrel, her body a quiver to take up the chase.

"Maggie." With the stern rebuke, the dog satisfied herself with a trot to the end of the leash, returned, and sat down next to Elizabeth.

Elizabeth strolled to the edge of the canal, Maggie close on her heels. The canal was still full of water but not rushing like the day before. Tracks dug in by the weight of the tow truck, led from the bank to the road. She could see the deep scar where her mail truck had landed in the soft mucky dirt on the other side. She looked down at the tracks, the smaller mail vehicle inside the tow truck grooves. The mail truck deposited heavy muck from the undercarriage as it bumped and strained against the chains of the larger tow truck.

Two gray squirrels ran across the grass behind Maggie. She caught sight of them and gave chase ripping her leash from Elizabeth's hand.

"Maggie, you come back here."

The dog disappeared into some bushes several yards away, barking as the squirrels climbed a tree chattering in excitement.

"Maggie, come!" Elizabeth called again.

Maggie emerged from the thicket, rolled on the grass with an object in her mouth. Dropping the thing, she pounced on it, gave it a chew, then ran to Elizabeth. The leash dragging behind her, she dropped her prize at her mistress's feet.

"Well, what did you find, girl?" Elizabeth grabbed the leash keeping a firm grip. "Looks like a man's black shoe. Yuk, it's filthy." She picked up the shoe, now with teeth marks and slobber, and quickly walked back to her vehicle. She let Maggie in the back, throwing the shoe on the floor next to her dog.

Elizabeth started the engine, gave it some gas, and turned left onto Red Snapper Lane. Completing the turn, she noticed the red flag was up on the first mailbox. "Now that's odd," she said. Maggie slithered forward on her stomach.

Elizabeth stopped, put the flag down and opened the box. Retrieving a white business-size envelope, she flipped the box closed and was about to press on the gas pedal when she noticed the envelope was addressed to her—Mail Lady.

"This is strange, Maggie. The Falcons are up in Maine for the summer. This isn't addressed to them, so I guess I can open it," she said and giggled. "I'm the only mail lady I know of here, wouldn't you say, girl?" Maggie replied with a faint bark. Elizabeth glanced over her shoulder at the house. It was the only house on the block where the mailbox was on the opposite side of the street.

Elizabeth opened the envelope and read the handwritten note.

"Dear Mail Lady, I'm sorry I couldn't stick around yesterday afternoon. I hope your lip wasn't cut too bad."

Chapter 7

———

"HELLO, LIZ? I'M CALLING from Atlanta."

"Hi, Mr. Goodwurthy. I—"

"Can you handle a job for me in the next couple of days?"

"Well, okay, Mr. Goodwurthy. Tell me what you need."

"Liz, for two years you've progressed from a green wannabe investigator to someone I can count on to get information fast. It's high time you call me Oliver. I have an urgent missing-person case. A frantic mother-of-the-bride called me. Her daughter's wedding is scheduled to take place, here in Atlanta, in five days."

"That's nice, Oliver."

"Yeah, well, the bride-to-be is missing."

"Oh, that's not so nice."

"To tell you the truth, Liz, if she were my mother, and I was getting married, I'd leave town, too."

"So, you want me to try to find her?"

"Yes, and the groom. I'm sending you a picture of the two of them. You can access your email from your phone?"

"Yes, go ahead. I'm on a mail run, but I'll take a look at my next break. What are their names?"

"Heather Bell and Charles Stanton, thirty-three and thirty-nine. Heather's first marriage and Stanton's second."

"Is there some reason you think they might be in this area?"

"Mrs. Bell happened to say that Heather and Charles spend all their free time going to bike shows, something Mrs. Bell sees as beneath her daughter. For the last three years, they have attended Biketoberfest in Daytona Beach."

"Oliver, that's two months away."

"Yes, but the wedding is in five days—maybe they decided to skip the big wedding and, well you get my drift."

"So, you think they might elope?"

"My thoughts exactly. Mrs. Bell, who is a bit neurotic but pays enough for me to put up with a few idiosyncrasies, tells me that if the wedding is going to be called off, it has to be done immediately—you know, church, band, dinners, yada yada."

"So you think they may plan to get married somewhere in the Daytona Beach area."

"Bingo. Keep a record of your time and expenses, and let me know what you find—hopefully, Heather and Charles."

"I'm on it."

It was time for Elizabeth's lunch break. She parked in her favorite spot shaded by large oak trees overlooking Spruce Creek River. Pulling out her cell phone from her purple and white tote, along with a bottle of water, and her mom's peanut butter and jelly sandwich, she quickly connected to the internet and found the telephone number from a website she'd heard of. The business offered wedding packages for bikers. Taking a bite of her sandwich, followed by a swig of water, she checked what a basic package offered. Closing the internet connection she then took a look at the picture of the happy couple that Oliver had emailed to her. Armed with their names and what they looked like, she called the number for the "Happy Bikers Forever, Your Wedding Today."

"Hello, Mrs. Boyd?"

"Yes, may I help you?"

"Oh, I hope so. I'm absolutely frantic. I'm supposed to meet my friend Heather, she's blonde, and her fiancé Charles for their very special day. But, Mrs. Boyd, I lost the slip of paper with the directions. Heather's going to kill me. Mrs. Boyd, by any chance, did they choose your services for the biggest day in their lives?"

"Oh, my dear, you are in luck. Of course, I offer the best wedding packages for bikers, quite famous really. My husband and I perform many weddings during bike week and—"

"Yes, Yes, that's exactly what Heather said."

"But Heather's request was a bit unusual, given it's August."

"Mrs. Boyd, you are a lifesaver. She was so excited about your white-lattice wedding package on the beach?" Elizabeth had seen this listed on the website and took a guess.

"That's it. The very one she chose."

"I remember her telling me about it. You know, how pretty it would be with the ocean in the background."

"Yes, and then they're having dinner at the Ocean Deck restaurant which is where we'll set up the lattice trellis. She said something about not too many of their friends knowing about their plans, so it was going to be small. Probably just three or four, so I'm sure she is going to be delighted you can make it. The groom is not sparing any expense. He reserved the honeymoon suite at the Hilton just down the road from where they'll be tying the knot."

"Wouldn't miss it for the world. It's tomorrow, I believe?"

"No, dear. Today. Six o'clock."

"Thank you, Mrs. Boyd. Rest assured I'll tell all my biker friends how wonderful you are to work with. Bye."

Elizabeth sent a text message to Oliver stating that she may have found the missing couple, closed her phone, and hastily finished her sandwich. Swallowing the last drop of water in her bottle, she turned her truck around and headed to her next mailbox.

"Well, Elizabeth you'd better get a move on. Seems you have a wedding to go to."

Chapter 8

———

ELIZABETH STUFFED THE FLYER into the last mailbox on her route. Finished, she dug into her tote and pulled out her cell phone.

"Hi, Dad. Maggie and I are on our way home. I'll just drop her off and—"

"Lizzy, that nice police officer called. He'd like you to drop by the morgue after work. He's wondering if you can ID the body."

"Okay. If he calls again tell him I'll go over as soon as I return my truck. See you in a few with Maggie. And, Dad, I have to go to an appointment beachside so I'll probably be a little late for dinner. Please go ahead without me." *Good thing I'm ahead of schedule,* she thought. *Two appointments at the same time will take some clever maneuvering.*

———

PUSHING THE DOOR OPEN to the medical examiner's office, Elizabeth was hit with a strong odor of chlorine permeating the frigid air. A man in a white coat, head bent down, a shock of silver-grey hair dangling over the edge of his glasses, looked up sharply to see who had invaded his space.

"Hello, young lady. Are you lost?"

"I'm looking for the medical examiner."

"That would be me, Sam Houston."

"I'm Elizabeth Stitchway. Detective Armstrong asked me to see you about the body he picked up at Turtle Grove Estates yesterday."

"Oh, my, yes. Miss Stitchway, you say?" he said offering his hand.

"Elizabeth Stitchway." Elizabeth said shaking his hand. She immediately liked the gentleman with his friendly blue eyes wrinkling at the corners as a smile spread across his cherubic face. She detected a slight English accent.

"Well, Elizabeth Stitchway, have you ever seen a corpse...a person fatally shot in the chest before?"

"No, I haven't, Mr. Houston. I plan to be a private investigator, so I think it's likely to go with the territory, so to speak."

"My, my, a private investigator. Well, let's go take a look at the body. See if you know who she is."

Elizabeth followed the coroner, his white coat fluttering a bit around his knees as he walked. Entering his laboratory, he escorted Elizabeth to a refrigerated area with a bank of drawers. Houston pulled one of the drawers out revealing a zippered bag.

"Before I show you the body, Miss Stitchway, let me say I put the woman in her mid-thirties. The autopsy is scheduled for tomorrow, so I'll know more about her after that. She apparently died from a bullet to the chest, probably through the heart. This won't be pleasant, Elizabeth. Many people called in to identify a corpse become sick to their stomach. There's a sink behind you if you should need it. Are you ready?"

"Yes, sir."

The coroner unzipped the bag from the head to the belly of the corpse. Elizabeth's stomach gave a slight lurch, and she felt the blood drain from her face. The coroner took a step toward her, but she waved him off. The frigid air, sterile atmosphere of the lab, and not recognizing the woman helped Elizabeth to keep from throwing up, or worse, to faint. Holding her ground, she thought that if she was going to be a PI, she'd better keep herself under control when seeing a dead person.

"I don't know her, sir. I'm sure I've never seen this woman before."

"As long as you're here, let me explain a few things," the coroner said. "You've heard of rigor mortis?"

"Yes, sir. But I do have a question. When I saw her bump into my mail truck, her arm that was dangling out of the wrapping seemed to move freely with the current. Why hadn't rigor mortis set in?"

"After death, the body becomes stiff, the result of rigor mortis. This commences about three hours after death and can take around twelve hours to complete maximum stiffness. But, and here is something most people don't know, about three days after death the stiffness gradually dissipates."

"So, she was in the water for at least three days?"

"Or, at least dead for that period of time."

"I think I've seen enough for now." Elizabeth backed away from the drawer, leaned over the sink for a minute, and then straightened up.

"Well done, Miss Stitchway." The coroner replaced the drawer and motioned Elizabeth to the door.

"Unless you have something else you want to ask me, I'll be leaving now, sir. Will you report back to Detective Armstrong that I didn't recognize the woman or should I call him?"

"I'll take care of it, Elizabeth. Thank you for stopping by."

Back in her car, Elizabeth pulled a cigarette from the pack in her glove compartment, lit up, took a long drag, and headed to the beach.

Chapter 9

———

HEARING A KNOCK ON the sunroom door, Joe flattened himself to the kitchen wall and peered around the corner.

"Hey, Joey. I know you're in there."

Someone was calling to him, but he couldn't make out who it was other than a man's silhouette against the late afternoon sun pouring through the glass.

"Joey, it's Gus. Gus Labrowski. Your best friend from Apalachee."

Apalachee? Apalachee Prison? No. It must be a trick.

"Joey, I seen you go in here. Now open the door."

Joe leaned closer. He took a good look. *God, it was Gus.* He strode to open the door. "Gus, I can't believe it. How did you find me? Quick, come in. I don't want anyone to know I'm here."

"Joey, you're a sight for sore eyes. How about a hug for your buddy?"

The two men embraced, laughing as they looked each other over.

"Gus, let's go in the kitchen, away from the windows. How did you find me?"

"Like a GPS gizmo. With everything you told me about your place here, it didn't take me long. If you remember I was paroled a few days before you were released. You and good behavior...that's a kick in the pants."

"Hey, I was a model prisoner. Want a beer?"

"Now I call that real hospitable of you. So this is the house your partner swindled you out of."

"This is it. What are you doing here, Gus?"

"I thought I might do a job for you."

"A job? I'm not in a position to hire anyone, not yet anyway."

"A job, you know, like I could take care of that bastard for you, so you could get your house back and get on with your life. I got this here gun, a real nice little .38 special." Gus pulled up his shirt to show Joe the gun stuck in his waistband.

"You're breaking your parole, man. If they catch you packing a weapon, you'll be back in prison before you can blink an eye."

"True, but they ain't gonna catch me. But you, Mister Upstanding Stockbroker, wouldn't want to get his fingers dirty. So, I'll take care of things for you."

"Gus, it's good to see you, glad you looked me up, but I have to take care of Walter Falcon myself. I think you can appreciate that it just wouldn't be as sweet if you took care of him. You know what I mean."

"Why are you getting all footsie with the mail lady in the mailbox? Your pal Gus can take care of things better than that little doll."

"I don't know what you're talking about."

"Oh, come on, Joey. This is Gus, your best bud, the one you dumped your guts out to every day in the yard."

"Honestly, Gus, I don't know what you mean."

"The two of you are passing love notes back and forth. I seen her stopping, and then you waiting until it's dark to see what sweet words she left for you in the mailbox."

"She has nothing to do with my plans to get Falcon."

"Okay, Joey. Whatever you say. I'm outta here for now. But just remember you can't trust a woman, and I'm watching your back. If she double crosses you, I'll take care of her. Here's my cell number, as in phone that is." Gus doubled over laughing at his joke. He tossed his empty can in the trash next to the sink, squeezed Joe's shoulder, and disappeared out the back door. Joe walked into the sunroom checking to make sure the door was locked. His foot touched something wet. He looked down and saw his soaked clothes where he had dropped them the night before. "Time to do a little housekeeping, son," he said setting his empty beer can on the table.

He picked up the mud-smeared shirt, pants, and windbreaker, put them in the washing machine, and pressed START.

"All the comforts of home."

Chapter 10

—

IT WAS A BEAUTIFUL evening for a wedding. Elizabeth walked through the Ocean Deck restaurant, down a narrow wooden staircase, and out the back entrance to the beach. Smack dab in front of her on the water's edge was a white-lattice arch, anchored with two planters on both sides, and the Atlantic Ocean serving as a backdrop. Twenty-four hours earlier the wedding would have taken place indoors.

A man sporting a white rose in the lapel of his white silk Harley Davidson shirt stood next to a blonde holding a bouquet of red and white roses. She wore a black leather sheath dress and matching black flip-flops. A woman with a salt and pepper bobbed haircut, held a bible. Another couple stood to the side. All were laughing.

Elizabeth strolled down to the gathering. "Hey, are you getting married?" she called out to the leather dress.

"Yes, we are. Want to be a witness? We need one more?"

"Sure," Elizabeth said. "I have a camera. Do you want me to take some pictures?" Elizabeth didn't wait for the answer snapping photos just in case the couple said no.

"That would be terrific," the blonde said, turning to the bible holder.

"I'm Elizabeth if I'm going to be a witness I guess I should know your names."

"I'm Heather Bell, and this is my soon-to-be-husband Charles Stanton. I hope you can join us for dinner after the ceremony. After all, you're now part of the wedding party."

"Thanks, I'd like to, but just for a drink to toast the new bride and groom. I have a date with my boyfriend. He doesn't like it when I'm late," Elizabeth said, winking at Heather.

Mrs. Boyd opened her bible and removed a folded piece of paper, smoothing it out so she could read it. And so the wedding took place.

The new Mrs. Stanton threw her bouquet to her friend, and then the couple walked up the beach to the restaurant, shaking the sand from their flip-flops before entering. Elizabeth excused herself to make a call.

"Oliver, I have everything."

"Liz, that breaks your record for finding a missing person. Give it to me."

"Heather Bell, now known as Heather Stanton, did, in fact, get married about twenty minutes ago. A lovely ceremony really."

"Cut the sarcasm, Stitchway."

"It was lovely. And, I was a witness. Check your email in an hour and you'll find a picture of the newlyweds."

"Do you know if they're spending the night in Daytona Beach?"

"Yup. The Hilton. I'm texting you the telephone number in case mummy wants to call and congratulate her daughter on her nuptials."

"I'm not sure I would want to hear that conversation. Good work, Elizabeth. Please include how you found them so fast in your report."

"HELLO, I'M HOME," Elizabeth called out. "Yes, Maggie, girl, I love you, too." Bending over, Elizabeth greeted the patient dog her tail sweeping the kitchen floor. Elizabeth gave her a scratch behind the ear and received a slurp on her cheek in return.

"Lizzy, I'm here, in the kitchen," Harry called out to his daughter. "Your mother is putting the finishing touches on a chicken stew."

Entering the kitchen, followed closely by Maggie, Elizabeth gave her mother a quick peck and took a taste of the stew gravy from the spoon her mother held out to her.

"Let me go wash up and send a quick email. I'll be back in a jiff."

Elizabeth went to her room, downloaded the wedding pictures from her camera, and sent them off to Oliver. She included a note with her report, asking him to let her know if Heather's mother decided to bury the hatchet in her new son-in-law's body. Smiling, she hit the send button and returned to the kitchen, sinking into her chair at the oak kitchen table.

"Mom, I asked dad to tell you I'd be late. Your stew tastes wonderful, and I'm starved."

"We decided to wait for you," Martha said.

"Hand me your glass, Lizzy, and I'll pour you a little wine. Now that the refrigerator is working, it's nice and cold. How did it go at the morgue? Did you recognize the body?"

"No. Umm, Dad, the wine tastes good. It turned out to be a woman just like the mystery man said. She didn't look too good, actually awful. The coroner thought she was probably in her mid-thirties. She had blonde hair. Looked tall. She was shot in the chest."

"Any sign of him, that mystery man, on your route today?" Martha asked.

"Nothing. But Maggie found a shoe. Hang on a minute. I threw it in the car."

Elizabeth and Maggie hustled out to the driveway retrieving the shoe from the trunk of the car.

"What do you think of this, Dad?" she asked handing the black leather shoe to her father.

"It's an expensive brand, and I see from the teeth marks that Maggie had some fun before she relinquished her new toy to you," Harry said, turning it over and inspecting the inside. "Looks to be slightly worn and, of course, full of mud. Where did Maggie find it?"

"Not far from where I landed in the canal. It was caught in some bushes. But that's not all I found today. Look at this." Elizabeth pulled out the envelope she had folded to fit in the pocket of her Capris.

"So he disappears when the police arrive, yet leaves me this note. What do you make of that, Mr. Retired Head of Security?"

"Now, dear," Martha said. "Let's not bring up that awful place."

"You're right, Mom. But, Dad, you're a real inspiration to me. After all, you started as a janitor on weekends in high school, then through college, and quickly rose to the head of security, in a big firm I might add. What's it been, two years since the accident?"

"Accident? My aching back. I was pushed over the stair railing from the third floor by somebody who had just threatened the president of the company. I was rushing up the stairs to help when this guy comes barreling down the stairwell throwing me out of his way. I was upended and hit the concrete floor below landing on my back. We never did catch him."

"Someday I'm going to find him, Dad. I know how hard it's been for you the past months," Elizabeth said putting her hand on his arm. "The operation, all those days in the hospital. But your company certainly treated you fairly—full insurance, plus disability income."

"Yes, they did. But you know, Martha," Harry said turning to his wife, "I'm going to be out of this chair sooner than you think. My therapist says it won't be long." Turning back to his daughter, laying his hand on hers, he said, "Elizabeth, you've been such a help to your mother and me. We're grateful you decided to move in with us when you did."

"Dad, that wasn't a hard decision. I didn't have a job."

"I guess we helped each other out." He took a sip of his wine, hesitated a few seconds, and cleared his throat. "Now, let me take a look at that piece of paper."

After reading the note, Harry slipped it back in the envelope. "I don't know what to make of this. But I do know you'd better keep your eyes and ears open and let's see where this man and the corpse lead you. Martha, hand me a knife and one of those little glass jars. I'm going to scrape a sample of the mud out of this shoe, and then Lizzy can wash it out."

"Yah. Evidence." Grinning, Elizabeth topped off her wine and nodded to her father asking if he would like more.

He pushed his glass to her. "Yes, please."

"You can wash that shoe off in the laundry sink out in the carport shed," Martha said, adding a handful of parsley to the stewpot.

"Where did you find the note?" Harry asked.

"8236 Red Snapper Lane. Dad, the flag was up, or I would never have stopped. The Falcons are snowbirds...go to Maine every summer. But with the red flag straight up, I stopped, and there it was. Maybe he just doesn't want to get involved. I looked at the Falcon's house across the street but didn't see any signs of them or a visitor. I suppose the man could live anywhere and just happened to pick box 8236."

"How did it go at the police station this morning and with Mr. Perkins," Martha asked. She sat down, handed her glass to her husband to pour some wine.

"Detective Armstrong asked me a few questions...mainly everything I told you and Dad last night. And, Mr. Perkins seemed a little out of sorts, but not mad, more annoyed at me. My vehicle was still in the shop, so he told me to drive number 923."

After dinner Elizabeth and her mother cleared the dishes and fell into their ritual performed after each meal—her mother washed, and she dried. They had a dishwasher but preferred to save money by doing it themselves.

They both liked the routine. It was a nice time for mother and daughter to share their day. Martha was rinsing the soapy water off a dinner plate when the phone rang.

Harry moved his chair under the wall phone. After a few pleasantries with the caller, Harry put his hand over the mouthpiece. "It's for you, Lizzy. Detective Armstrong."

"Hello, Detective...no, I didn't spot the man, but I did get a note. It was in box 8236. No, he wasn't around. I think he just happened to put it in that mailbox."

Elizabeth picked up a plate, absentmindedly dried it as the detective talked the phone tucked under her chin.

"He wrote he was sorry he had to leave and hoped that my lip was okay...no, he didn't sign it. Yes, I'll let you know if I see him. Bye."

———

ELIZABETH REPLACED THE RECEIVER on the wall hook and turned to her father. "So, what do you think I should do about the shoe and, more important, the note?"

Chapter 11

———

A SLIVER OF THE morning sun struck Joe in the eyes through a crack in the window shade. He turned his head away. "How wonderful...sun in my eyes." He turned back to feel the heat on his cheek.

Abruptly throwing off the thin sheet, he sprang from the bed and performed some knee bends. He caught his image in the full-length mirror. "Not too bad, Joe, my boy." He raked his sandy-brown hair with his fingers, stooping a little so his six-foot-one frame fit in the mirror. Tilting his head, he caught his dark-blue eyes looking back at him. His entire body was lily white—he looked like a northerner. The Florida sun would soon turn the lily white to a golden brown.

Joe headed down the hall in his bare feet. Stopping at the thermostat, he set it to seventy-four degrees, smiling when he heard the AC kick in. *How great is that—I can control the temperature of the air on my skin.* Dressed only in his jockey shorts, he continued on to the kitchen.

Sunshine filtered through the drawn shades filling the house with a soft light. All the walls in the house were white. Oriental throw rugs softened the white tile floors with the exception of some carpeted rooms—the bedrooms and office.

The house was silent.

Joe wasted no time starting the coffeemaker. *Strange,* he thought, *almost two years in jail and the coffee and filters are still where I kept them.* With the music of percolating coffee following him, he returned to the bedroom. He pulled out the bottom drawer of the dresser. Not finding what he wanted, he pulled out another drawer and selected a pair of tan shorts. Then to the closet. Shuffling hangers, he picked out a white golf shirt. Dressing in the clean clothes, he left his feet bare strolling back to the kitchen, the aroma of fresh-brewed coffee beckoned him.

Taking a sip, he looked out the glass door of the sunroom to the side yard, the street, and the canal beyond. "Another idyllic day in paradise. Hard to believe the violence of the hurricane," he said quietly to himself, savoring the sound of his voice without the clanging of cell doors banging shut in the background.

Retrieving his coffee, he strode down the hall to the office. His bare feet muffled his footfall on the tile and then silence as he entered the carpeted room.

Joe looked straight at the painting behind the gleaming cherry desk. A friend of his who knew his fixation with pelicans had painted a scene on the intracoastal river with a weathered dock in the foreground. Several white pelicans were preening in the morning sun.

Joe walked behind the desk, felt for the latch under the heavy gilt frame swinging it away from the wall. He twisted the combination lock—left, right, left again. At the slight sound of a click, the heavy safe door swung back to his touch.

"Oh, Walt. How stupid you are. You not only didn't change the combination, but you also left me your mad money. How very thoughtful." Joe fanned the bills guessing he now had enough money, over eighty grand, to fund his revenge.

"Okay, asshole, let's see what else you left hanging around." What Joe really wanted to uncover was proof that Walter Falcon had framed him.

Two hours later, after meticulously going through every scrap of paper in the office, Joe headed to the master bedroom.

"Oh, yah, the room of unabated wild love. What a joke. You never saw a skirt you didn't want to get under. Hope you enjoyed yourself." He pulled open the drawer of the nightstand—eye drops, nail file, some tissues. He went to the other side of the bed and pulled out a pack of Trojans from under a book on the art of sailing. "Well, well, Walter. Does Mona know about these?"

Joe continued searching the room rifling through all the dresser drawers, but carefully returning the items exactly the way he found them. Lying on the floor, he peered under the bed. The mattress was only inches off the carpet so he couldn't scooch under. He pulled all the bedding away—maroon, white and tan striped quilt, tan blanket, the white sheets, and pillows. He removed the thick quilted pad and a rubber sheet. He stared at the mattress, not believing what he saw. He lifted the top mattress and reached underneath. Feeling around, his hand touched a small object. Picking it up, he let the mattress fall back over the box springs. He then reassembled the bedding.

It was after three o'clock, the time the mail lady stopped the day before. He had seen her pick up his note, look over at the house, and then drive on. *I probably missed her,* he thought. Nevertheless, he hustled to the front window, carefully moving one of the blinds back just enough to see out. The street was empty. Pulling his head away he heard her truck and looked again. *She must be running late. She's driving fast...didn't even slow down at 8236.*

He watched her stop at the mailbox up the lane, and then the next.

"What the? She's getting out of her truck."

———

ELIZABETH PICKED UP THE package for Mrs. Stedly. Too big for the mailbox, she turned off the motor, put on the handbrake, and hustled up to the front door. She rang the doorbell, placed the package by the door, and started to turn away. Stopping in her tracks, she tilted her head, listening. *Did someone say help?* She took a step back to the door.

"Mrs. Stedly, are you there?" Again she thought she heard a faint call for help. Scooting behind a bush to the right of the front door, she put her hands up to her eyes and peered through the window pane. She could just make out a foot from behind a chair.

"Oh, my God, Mrs. Stedly are you hurt?" Again she heard a faint call for help. Darting back to the front door, she tried the latch. Locked. She ran around the side of the house, turned the knob to the back door. It was unlocked, and Elizabeth stepped in.

"Mrs. Stedly I'm coming...I'm coming," she called out as she made her way to the front of the house.

"Here...in the hall," came a soft voice, no more than a whisper.

"Oh, Mrs. Stedly, did you fall?"

There was no response from the woman lying on the red hall-carpet runner. Elizabeth took a few steps to the living room, grabbed the tan blanket covering the back of the couch. After laying the blanket over Mrs. Stedly, she pulled the cell phone out of her Capris and dialed 911.

"Hello, I'm a mail carrier. I just found a woman lying unconscious in the hallway of her home, the address is 8246 Red—"

"We have your location. Is the woman still conscious?"

"Yes."

"An ambulance has been dispatched. Do you know CPR?"

"Yes, yes."

"Is there anyone in the house who can help you?"

"No. She lives alone."

"Turn her on her back. Check for a pulse. If you can't feel it, put your cheek next to her nose. Is she breathing?"

"Yes, yes, she is."

———

JOE SAW THE MAIL LADY look in the window of the house and then watched as she ran around the side and disappeared. An ambulance rounded the corner heading up Red Snapper Lane. Three medics scrambled out of the vehicle and ran up the driveway, one carrying a case. The front door opened and they went inside. Several minutes later two men returned to the ambulance, retrieved a gurney, and went back into the house.

Shortly, Joe saw them bring someone out and load the person into the ambulance. At the same time, the mail lady emerged from the house, closed the door, and appeared to check if it was locked. The ambulance pulled away, and the mail lady walked briskly to the house next door,

talked with someone standing on the front steps. She motioned to the house where the medics

had left with someone on a stretcher, backed away a few steps, and then returned to her mail truck. He continued to watch until she was out of sight, disappearing around the curve of the road.

Joe, returning to his search for evidence, ambled through the rest of the house, eyes seeking any type of storage place where Falcon might keep important documents. Back in the kitchen, he stuffed a couple of items into his pants pocket, pulled out the coffee can and another filter. All in all, it had been a very productive day. He didn't find everything he was looking for, but there were a few surprises. He saw the mail lady responding to some kind of an emergency, again. A smile crossed his face as he pushed the ON button of the coffeemaker. The soft music of the brewing coffee once again floated through the kitchen.

Chapter 12

―――

"WELCOME TO CHANNEL 13 news at noon.

Police report a woman's body was found in a drainage canal located in Turtle Grove Estates, Port Orange, during the hurricane two days ago. Cause of death was not revealed, but a lady mail carrier found the unidentified body. The force of the wind overturned her mail truck and landed on its side in the same canal.

As of this report, the dead woman is listed as Jane Doe.

Detective Armstrong, Port Orange Police Department, did say he would give us an update as soon as more information is available.

Now for the traffic report."

―――

"SO, THEY FOUND HER. Damn hurricane must have flushed her out of the pipe. Oh well, it was bound to happen sooner or later."

Chapter 13

———

ELIZABETH SLIPPED ON HER favorite sandals, orange jellies with red rhinestones dotting little yellow flowers. Her red curls pulled back tight into a ponytail poked through the hole in back of her yellow-billed cap keeping her hair off her neck in the hot, humid air. Thankfully, her route was residential—no uniform required. She knew the bright colors kept her mood upbeat, something that was hard for a carrier being alone in a vehicle all day. She rarely wore makeup—her big brown eyes were already fringed with thick lashes. But she did apply a stroke of lip gloss because she said her lips dried out even in the summer months. Satisfied she had what she needed, Elizabeth bolted out the front door, giving Maggie a pat on the head as she swept by.

"Bye, Dad. I'm off to work."

Harry wheeled himself behind the screen door and waved to his daughter. He watched her climb into her yellow Ford coupe, the vintage car he bought off a used car lot. His plans to restore it for a son someday were altered when his daughter was born. When he first held his baby girl with the curly red hair, he knew she was going to be a natural behind the wheel of the little car. He couldn't help but chuckle as he watched the cheery rainbow of colors surrounding his pot of gold back the coupe out of the driveway.

———

ELIZABETH SETTLED BEHIND THE wheel of her own sparkling mail truck, number 328. The workmen at the repair shop had outdone themselves with their wash job. Skirting around cleanup crews to the start of her route, she heard motorized saws, and the engines of bulldozers straining to push uprooted trees into piles. Lines of city dump trucks followed the crews, picking up the piles of debris left behind by the hurricane. Port Orange was getting back to normal.

The hot summer sun beat down on the workers, and the moisture in the air sent the humidity skyrocketing. Elizabeth's T-shirt stuck to her body. Her sweat making the already vivid colors—*Daytona Beach* stenciled over a bright orange sun rising from the blue ocean—even brighter. Her shorts matched the orange of the sun on her shirt.

The man's shoe, now free of mud, was wrapped in a plastic bag in the bottom of her apple-green backpack along with a peanut butter and jelly sandwich, three bottles of water, and a few of her mom's chocolate chip cookies. This morning there was another item in the pack—a note addressed to the mystery man.

Friday's mail was always heavy with additional flyers alerting residents to the weekend bargains they just couldn't live without. She was forced to drive a little slower than usual because of all the heavy equipment darting in and out of side streets. She was later than normal when she started her route at 11:20.

Driving through the network of roads that crisscrossed inside Turtle Grove Estates, she saw more trucks and the sounds of the power saws were louder as she methodically inched along between the mailboxes. A few of the boxes were still lying on the ground, the victims of shooting palm fronds or lawn furniture hurled against them.

"Hi, Mr. Fowler. I see you have Sam on the treadmill. Sure was a nasty storm wasn't it?"

"Certainly was, Elizabeth. I don't dare take Sam for a walk. She's scared of all the loud noises from the heavy equipment."

"I didn't think that big red Doberman of yours would be scared of anything. Bye."

"Hi, Theresa. Not much mail for you today...just a few flyers."

"Thank you, dear. Did you get caught in that hurricane? It rolled in so fast...even though the weatherman told us it was coming. This is the first day I dared to venture out of the house."

"I sure did. My mail truck was blown into a canal. I only had a few deliveries left but I'm pretty sure I saved a good portion of the mail. Bye."

Hearing her cell phone music, Elizabeth parked off to the side of the road, dug in her shorts pocket, pulling out her phone. Checking the caller ID, she flipped it open.

"Hi, Dad. What's up?" Elizabeth never talked on her phone when she was working unless she felt it was an emergency. Because of the day her dad fell down the stairs at work, seriously injuring his back, she always answered her parent's call.

"Lizzy, I wanted to let you know the noon news just reported the body you found in the canal."

"Did they give my name?"

"No, only that a lady mail carrier discovered it."

"Did they say anything about the mystery man?"

"Not a word."

"Okay, thanks, Dad. See you tonight."

Several of her clients—Elizabeth liked to think of them that way because she felt she was providing a professional service—were either waiting for her or rushed out of their houses after her delivery. A quick chitchat about the storm with those waiting at their boxes and then she was on to the next address.

"They must not have heard the news yet. I sure don't want to talk to everyone about the body, or I'll never finish my deliveries."

Gray squirrels bolted back and forth across the road. "Poor things. They're upset over the storm and now the noise of the cleanup crews," she said to herself. Fact is Elizabeth talked nonstop while she worked keeping herself company.

"I wonder if I'll see the mystery man today? Oh, little turtle, I see you," she said tapping her brakes. "Red Snapper Lane's just ahead. Time to turn left, Elizabeth. Yup, there's the mailbox." She stopped next to box 8236. Reaching for her backpack, she pulled out her last water bottle, the shoe, and the envelope with the note she and her dad had written the night before. Her plan was to leave the shoe in the mailbox along with the note, just in case it belonged to the mystery man. She knew that as expensive as her dad said it was, no man would want to be left without the mate.

Taking the white handsome note card with a raised edge out of the envelope, she checked it one last time.

> *Mystery Man,*
> *My lip is mending nicely. Thank you for asking.*
> *Maggie, my dog, found this shoe in the brush near where I was blown into the canal. My dad says it's very expensive. I'm leaving it with this note in case you lost it.*
> *Thanks for your help. I don't know where you live, so I hope you get this message.*
> *Sincerely,*
> *Mail Lady*

"Okay, Mr. Mystery Man, here's the shoe. I'll just stand the note inside. The shoe certainly is big enough to hold it." Satisfied with how she positioned the shoe in the mailbox, Elizabeth pushed the door up and gave it an extra tap to be sure it was closed tight. Stepping on the gas pedal, she drove on to the next box.

———

JOE SAW THE MAIL truck stop at box 8236. When the vehicle moved down the road, he dropped the shade back into place. He didn't want anyone to know he was in the house. He had spent the day searching for documents, any kind of document that might clear him of all the embezzlement charges. His search was in vain.

Frustrated and feeling cabin fever set in, he dragged out Falcon's bicycle from the garage, through the house into the sunroom. With the oak trees and dense palmetto bushes surrounding the perimeter of the backyard providing cover, he slid the bicycle out the sunroom door, across the lawn to a small hole in the vegetation. Steering the bike through the opening, he was instantly on the sidewalk of the main street that circled through Turtle Grove Estates. No houses faced this street, so he became just another homeowner out riding his bike.

The large pocket in his knee-length tan shorts was held closed with Velcro protecting his money clip. With the bills in his pocket, thanks to Walter, Joe headed out to buy a motorcycle. He knew he didn't dare risk buying a car. The garage of his house opened onto Red Snapper Lane with houses on either side. Someone would surely see him. While many of the neighbors were snowbirds, there were a few who lived on his street year-round.

"As soon as it's dark, I'll check the mailbox. She stopped. Maybe she was checking to see if I left another note."

Joe pedaled out of the development the breeze billowing under his black tank top. He headed east to a Harley dealer three miles away.

Chapter 14

———

"HEY, HELEN, ANY PLANS for the weekend?"

"You bet I have. Deliver this stuff as fast as I can and head home. My husband bought tickets to the Daytona Cubs baseball game. They're playing local, at the Jackie Robinson ballpark."

"Sounds like fun. See you Monday."

Elizabeth picked up the bundles of mail for her route. Saturday was usually a light day, and she was anxious to pack her truck and head out of the post office yard. The sooner she finished her run the sooner she'd get home and help her dad with his exercises. She pushed her half-full cart through the swinging doors, waved to a couple of co-workers, and packed her bundles into number 328. Even though the mail was lighter on Saturday morning, the traffic always slowed her down because of the crazy shoppers speeding, switching lanes trying to beat a crowd for retailer's Saturday specials. Several mail vans had pulled out of the yard at the same time she did. They looked like a game of follow-the-leader traveling in a line down Dunlawton Avenue. One by one they peeled off to the beginning of their routes. Elizabeth led the parade and was the only mail truck left as she turned into Turtle Grove Estates.

"Well, Elizabeth, I wonder if the mystery man left you a note today? Maybe the shoe will still be in the mailbox, or maybe he didn't even check."

"Hey, Mrs. Trent, you're making good time this morning."

"Hi, Elizabeth. Trying to burn a few fat cells before our big Sunday dinner. The whole family. See you later."

"Yah. Bye." Elizabeth drove on down the road. "Run off her Sunday dinner...like she really needs to jog every day. The skinny thing."

Elizabeth continued on her route, shouting out short pleasantries to her clients along the way. With the light Saturday load and the numerous snowbirds, who had their mail forwarded, she made good time. She hummed as she bumped along enjoying the beautiful, sunny, hot morning.

"Elizabeth, maybe it's time you decided on your future...like your next move. Dad sounded like he'd be up and walking soon. My last missing-person case for Oliver—Goodwurthy Private Investigators— was fun and sooo easy. Googling a couple of keywords and up popped Mrs. Boyd's Biker Wedding website. Heather probably did the same thing—no need to call anyone else. If I worked a few more years full time for Oliver, I could open my own office...or not. Whoa, watch out, mister."

Reaching for the bag of cookies next to her, she kept her eyes fixed on the road. She had to be careful of the dump trucks still hauling debris away, but the sounds of power saws had diminished markedly over the past couple of days. Many of her clients were out cleaning up their yards, creating giant piles of tree limbs by their curbs. City crews would stop by later and pick up the damage left behind by the seventy-plus-miles-per-hour winds.

Stopping by a mailbox, deposited two circulars and reached down for her navy-blue tote before moving on. Retrieving the last bottle of water, she took a long swallow followed by a cookie and another drink of water. She brushed the crumbs off her conservative yellow-daisy flowered shirt over navy and white striped shorts. For some reason, she put her hand on the back of her neck feeling a cool breeze or was it the sensation that she was being watched? Dismissing the notion, she took note that no one was coming up behind her, she was on her way with a pump on the gas pedal, humming again as she neared the canal, making the left turn onto Red Snapper Lane. "Let's see what 8236 holds for me today, if anything. The flag is up a little, but not like before," she mused, squinting to see better in the strong afternoon sun.

Elizabeth pulled down the door to the mailbox. At first, she thought it was empty—no shoe, no note. But putting her face to the opening, peering inside, she saw at the very back was a white business-size envelope, same as before, addressed to "Mail Lady."

"My, my, let see what he has to say today." She slit the envelope with her ruby-red fingernail and pulled out a sheet of paper folded in thirds.

> *Dear Mail Lady,*
> *I'm glad to hear that your lip is healing. The way it was bleeding I knew the cut was probably deep, maybe even requiring stitches.*
> *I need some help, and I was wondering if you would be so kind to meet me at the new Spruce Creek Recreation Center tomorrow morning. I'm sure you know where it is—you must pass it every day. Say 10:00? I would rather talk to you about my request than write it out.*
> *Please thank Maggie for finding my shoe. Bring her with you, and I'll find you in the dog park.*
> *Maybe I can clear up some of the mystery around Mystery Man.*
> *Vincent*

She refolded the letter, tucked it back into the envelope, and looked over at the house. "Now, what do you make of that, Elizabeth? It sure doesn't look like anybody's living there. Maybe he's a friend of the Falcons."

———

HARRY YANKED HIS WHEELCHAIR to the kitchen table. "I don't like the thought of your meeting a strange man all alone, even if it is in the park," Harry said.

"Dad, I'm not a kid."

"That's what worries me. You're a very pretty young woman."

"I'll have my cell phone, and besides do you know how many people take their dogs to the dog park on Sunday morning? Let me tell you—lots. And I won't be alone because Maggie will be with me. The city fixed a real nice place for dogs to run."

Maggie immediately sat down next to Elizabeth, ears up, tail dusting the linoleum floor.

Elizabeth nuzzled her dog's neck. "Yes, I'm talking about you. You'll protect me from the big bad boogie man won't you?" Maggie gave Elizabeth a slurp in the ear. "Dad, I'll be fine. Besides aren't you just a little curious as to why he needs help?"

"Of course, I'm curious. But I'm more concerned about your welfare. How about your mother and I drop you and Maggie off and wait in the car? Then if you scream bloody murder, I'll hear you?"

"Absolutely not!"

Chapter 15

———

ELIZABETH TURNED INTO THE parking area of the Spruce Creek recreation facility and parked her yellow coupe. Looking in the rearview mirror, she refreshed her tomato-red lipstick and tucked a loose curl behind her ear. Stepping out of her car, she smoothed her NASCAR T-shirt down over her red shorts. "Looks like lots of doggie friends for you, Maggie girl. You'll have to mind your manners."

Shouldering her macramé bag, Elizabeth leaned into the car, picked up Maggie's leash and gave a little tug. Maggie jumped out the driver's side of the car and shook her furry body from head to tail. It was a little before ten o'clock, but Elizabeth looked around for Vincent anyway. "You know, Maggie, I hope I recognize him. I only saw him for a short time...and with the wind and rain in my eyes—"

"Hello there, Mail Lady. And this must be Maggie. Thanks for finding my shoe, pretty girl." The man stooped over giving the dog a good rub behind her ears. Maggie's tail waved rapidly in appreciation. Lurching forward she knocked him to the ground.

"Maggie, no! I'm sorry. She generally doesn't get so excited especially meeting someone for the first time."

"Not a problem," he said laughing. "It's nice to be greeted, shall we say, with exuberance."

"Are you Vincent? I mean you must be. You're taller than I remember, but then I don't remember much. Excuse me for rattling on, but you look different, not so—"

"Bedraggled?"

Elizabeth was a bit distracted by this man looking down into her eyes with an easy smile crossing his face.

"Do you want to take Maggie over to the dog park?" he asked.

"I suppose so. No, wait. Let's walk along the nature trail."

"Alright. I'd like to stop calling you Mail Lady. May I ask your name?"

"Well, you did practically save my life. My name is Elizabeth, Elizabeth Stitchway. What's your last name, Vincent?"

"It's Price. Vincent Price. Would you like some coffee? I picked up a couple of cups for us."

Elizabeth nodded that she would.

"Let me just grab the bag."

"That's very thoughtful don't you think, Maggie?" She whispered.

Vincent jogged to his Harley, removed the cups from the bag and returned to Elizabeth. "I have creamers in my pocket and sugar. Do you take either one in your coffee?"

"Yes, please. That would be nice—cream, no sugar." Elizabeth felt she was behaving oddly, but he was so nice. She found herself relaxing, her lips forming a little smile as he fished out the creamers from his short cargo pants.

"Here, let me open that for you, your hands are full. One or two?"

"Two, thanks." Maggie sat beside Elizabeth watching the man, ears up, tongue hanging out panting in the heat of the sun.

"And, Maggie, here's a biscuit for you. A little token of my appreciation for finding my shoe."

Maggie quickly stood, carefully taking the biscuit from his fingers, chewed once and it was gone.

"That was very nice of you, Vincent."

He apparently didn't hear her. He walked back to his bike and pulled a few napkins from the bag.

"I said that was very nice of you, Vincent."

Returning, he handed a napkin to her. "Now that we're armed with our morning cup of joe let's hit that nature trail you mentioned."

They strolled over to a small bridge next to a sign—Nature Trail Starts Here. The bridge led to a path bordered on both sides by arching oak trees and tall pines. Palmetto bushes were thick on each side. Pine needles covered the path. Maggie, nose to the ground, checked every opening between and under the bushes and gave a soft whine when a squirrel jumped overhead from one branch to another.

"She sure is a well-behaved dog. Most dogs would be barking by now."

"She has her moments. Sometimes I take her in my truck and barking is definitely a no-no."

They came to another narrow bridge, this time spanning a trickle of a stream running underneath. Elizabeth leaned against the weathered railing taking a sip of coffee.

They looked up as a young boy and girl, both towheads, careened toward the narrow bridge on their bicycles.

"I'll beat you, Samantha."

"No you're won't. Get out of my way. Watch out."

Samantha's front tire rammed his bike sending her bike into the bushes. Vincent, Elizabeth, and Maggie ran to help her. Crying, Samantha wiped blood from her elbow onto her black shorts as Maggie kissed a tear from her face.

"Here, let me help you up," Vincent said lifting the child out of the bushes. "That's a nasty cut on your elbow." He pulled a handkerchief from his shorts pocket and wrapped it around the little girl's cut. "That should hold you until you get home. Do you live near here?"

"Yes, sir. The other side of the park. That was my brother."

"Here's your bike," Elizabeth said, wheeling it onto the path and pulling a bottle of water from her shoulder bag. "How about I wash those tear smudges away?" Elizabeth, smiling as she doused a paper napkin with the water, washed the little girl's face. "Now, I think you'd better ride home and let your mother clean that cut."

"Thanks. What's your dog's name?"

"Maggie."

"She sure is nice. Thanks for the water. Bye."

Elizabeth walked back to the bridge and retrieved her coffee. "Boy's can be so mean."

"Well, she did ram into him."

"Now let's get to it, Vincent," Elizabeth said dismissing his remark. "Are you friends of the Falcons? And what did you mean when you wrote that you needed my help?"

He leaned against the rail on the opposite side. Looked into the trees and took a long sip of his coffee. Turning to face Elizabeth, he looked straight into her eyes.

"In answer to your first question, yes I know the Falcons. I'm staying in their house for a few days, or maybe a couple of weeks. Which brings me to your second question. I haven't been able to reach Walter and Mona. They must be in Maine, or maybe vacationing out of the country. I would like to know when they plan to return to Port Orange for the winter. I'm presuming November, but it might be sooner. I'm sure they left a card with the post office with instructions to forward their mail. Can you take a look to see when they plan to return and let me know? If they're coming sooner, I want to be sure to leave the house in good order."

"Good heavens, I can't do that. That card is private post office information. It would totally be against regulations."

"Well, just the month would be helpful. Can you at least do that?"

"It's against reg—"

"I know. I know. It's against regulations. Well, if the card just happens to fall in your lap, please stop by the house. The back door will be ajar. I know from the last couple of days that you pass by the house around three in the afternoon."

"Why the back door? Why not the front?"

"I'm usually working back there. That's why."

"Okay, you don't have to get huffy. What kind of work do you do, you know, for a living?"

"I'm, or was, a stockbroker. My own company."

"Is there a missus stockbroker."

"You've got to be kidding. There's no time for women. They make demands...want a guy to do stuff...stuff he may not want to do. Okay to have a woman, excuse me, a date once in a while, but a wife— never. You certainly are a nosey one. What are you, some kind of a detective?"

"Look, you asked me to meet you here. I didn't just come looking for you, and yes, I'm a private investigator. Almost."

"Almost? You're either a PI, or you're not? Which is it?"

"I'm planning on opening my own business soon. Real soon."

"Well, Miss Stitchway, PI, did the police identify that body you found?"

"I found? I believe we both saw it and you dragged it out of the water before you pulled a Houdini."

"So, has the body been identified?"

"The coroner asked me to come over to see if I knew her, the body. And, no, I didn't recognize her. It was a woman, just as you thought. When I was there, the coroner hadn't performed an autopsy. But he said she was shot. In the chest. He told me there weren't any marks on her body. But she was obviously murdered."

"Why is that?"

"For a stockbroker, you sure aren't too bright. If she killed herself, how would she wrap herself up in a blanket and then end up in the canal?" Thrusting her fist into her bag, Elizabeth pulled out a cigarette, a matchbook, and lit up.

Vincent quickly stepped in front of her, carefully removed the cigarette from her lips and ground it out with his heel. "Hasn't anyone told you smoking is bad for your health?"

"Hey, if I want to smoke I'll smoke."

"Even if there's a no smoking sign on this trail?"

"Come on, Maggie, time for us to go."

"Wait. How about another cup of coffee? There's an ice cream parlor across the street. I haven't talked to anyone...face to face...for awhile."

"No thanks. Mags and I are finished here." Elizabeth, Maggie trotting after her, started to walk back along the path. She turned and looked directly at him. "By the way, mister, no way is your name Vincent Price. He's been dead for seventeen years, and you are nowhere near as sinister as the guys he played in the movies. And the handkerchief that you put around the little girl's elbow was monogrammed with an F."

———

JOE WATCHED THE WOMAN with curly red hair strut back to her car, her dog at her heel. *Now there goes the reason a man should remain a bachelor. Maybe a fling now and then, but I'll stick to my motto— no more than three dates. After that, they think they own you.*

Picking up Elizabeth's cigarette butt, he deposited it in the trash barrel on his way back to his motorcycle. He looked over at the exit road and watched the yellow coupe turn out of the park.

Chapter 16

———

MONA, STANDING INSIDE THE living room protected by thermo-pane glass, watched her husband out on the terrace. She loved their summer home, a tranquil retreat from the tensions which always surrounded her life in Florida. She hugged her body, listening to the beat of the ocean waves in front of their property. No matter how many times Walter yelled, the sound of the waves soothed her.

She spent hours sitting in the sun on the flagstone terrace reading or daydreaming about her life, how nice it might be if they could stay year round in Maine. Her wardrobe was made of three looks—bathing suits for sunning, filmy caftans for lounging, and smart Capris with various jeweled tops for shopping. She felt feminine and beautiful in all of them.

This morning she appeared as fragile as a little doll in her pale-blue silk caftan, her blonde hair cascading down her back. It was a sensual illusion she took great pains to portray in front of her husband, who had a wandering eye. However, underneath the silky garment was a body hardened from hours of swimming in the ocean, or if the seas were too rough, then lap after lap in their heated pool.

Walter Falcon slammed his cell phone shut, throwing it across the stone terrace. Skittering on the bumpy surface, the phone slammed into the door frame.

"Mona. Mona. Where the hell are you? Come out here. Smitty just called."

Moving slowly, ghost-like, out to her bellowing husband, Mona picked up the instrument that had facilitated his irritation and set it down on the glass table under the shade of a green umbrella.

"Walter, stop your screaming. Whatever Smitty said can't warrant your screaming. Calm down."

Walter didn't look at his wife as she joined him on the terrace. "I'm not screaming." He stared out over the shoreline of his Ogunquit home. He stood rigid, his body tanned from the hours he spent sailing his boat. He kept physically fit, a fanatic about his workout routine. His clients seeking advice on how to invest their money knew him to be a warm counselor, one who spent hours helping them maximize their portfolios—on the clock. Always on the clock. He was careful to bill them for every minute of his precious expertise.

Walter raised his gaze. A freighter was making its way through the icy waters of the Atlantic, but he didn't see the ship. All he could see was the image of his former partner and the hatred in Joe's eyes when the judge announced the verdict: "Guilty. Perhaps three years behind bars, Mr. Joseph Sinclair Rockwell, AKA Mr. Rocket, will cause you to think twice before embezzling money again from your business partner." The gavel crashed down on the heavy oak block. Joe yelled out that he would get him someday. Walter had no doubt that Joe would try to exact his revenge. He had to remain on guard so that didn't happen.

Walter's body jerked, still hearing the gavel, a year and a half later. In his dreams, or awake, he saw Joe's eyes and heard the crack of the gavel, always the crack of the gavel.

"Walter, I asked you, what did Smitty say?" Mona asked again in a soft voice.

Walter abruptly turned to his wife. "I'll tell you what he said" He spat out the words like snake venom. "Joe was released from prison five days ago."

"Oh, no," Mona whispered, her hands moving to her throat. "But it's only been a year and a half. How could he—"

"Time off for good behavior. Good behavior. That's a good one."

"Does Smitty know where he is? You said Joe threatened you."

"No. The asshole lost him. Mona, we have to make a quick trip to Port Orange. Throw our stuff together—enough for three days on the road. We'll just stay a few days. I have to check the house...change the locks. We'll come right back here."

"No, no, I don't want to go back to the house. Not yet."

"Have it your way. I'll go alone."

"Oh sure, Walter. Who will it be this time? A brunette? Or maybe redhead?"

Chapter 17

———

ELIZABETH'S SHOULDERS SLUMPED at the sight of sacks of mail lined up at her station. Mondays were always heavy, but because of the storm, the trucks from the distribution centers had been delayed. During the night they had arrived non-stop dropping off more and more bags of mail as they struggled to catch up. There was no chitchat between the carriers today. Everyone had their head down. Helen had a snarly look on her face and didn't look up when Elizabeth whizzed by her.

On top of the extra bags to be sorted, the AC wasn't keeping up with the day's ninety-five degrees heat, and the heavy humidity still lingered from the storm. Standing still at her table, not moving a muscle, Elizabeth could feel her skin sweat, the bouquet of red and yellow tulips on her T-shirt wilted as the cloth dampened.

She turned and headed back to the receiving desk. "Hi, Bob. Can I have my mail-forwarding cards? With the piles of stuff I have, I want to be sure I don't screw up."

Striding back to her station, Elizabeth thumbed through the yellow cards hesitating only a moment as she passed the Falcon's instructions—Forward all First Class Mail as of June 23 to 78 Glenn Cove Circle, Ogunquit, Maine. Resume Delivery October 5 to 8236 Red Snapper Lane, Port Orange, Florida.

Tackling the first bag of mail, she heaved it up on the table and dumped out the contents. *I'm supposed to be strong enough to lift seventy pounds. That one felt more like a hundred.*

Putting the Falcon's forwarding information out of her mind, Elizabeth quickly started her sorting routine. She knew she was one of the fastest at this part of the operation. One particularly slow day a while back word spread through the carriers about a contest to see who could be out the door first. Everyone was supposed to start at exactly 8:15. The first one done would call out *snake bite*. Elizabeth had yelled first. She smiled to herself thinking of that morning—anything to keep her mind off the humidity.

This morning, she wasn't the first by a long shot. Several of the carriers with shorter runs had already packed their vehicles and were driving out of the yard. Elizabeth's bin was piled high, some of the letters spilling over to the concrete floor. She darted down the aisle, rolling a second bin up to her station. Two bins resulted in her making two trips through the swinging doors to the back of her truck. At last, she was packed and ready to leave. She drove out of the yard and turned right onto Dunlawton Avenue.

Fortunately, by the time she was on the road the business traffic had already gone through. Cleanup crews, hanging onto the backs of huge dump trucks, were still on the road, but today

at least there were fewer of them. Port Orange maintenance was almost back to normal. Various vans, decorated with signs stating the type of work the owner engaged in, were replacing the bulldozers. Roofers, builders, and painters were out giving estimates to weary homeowners. The Stitchways were participants in this play. Harry had an appointment in the afternoon with a handyman to repair his carport.

Elizabeth could feel her body relaxing as she drove the two miles to the beginning of her route. Opening her yellow backpack on the floor to her left side, she pulled out one of the water bottles.

"Already warmed up, aren't you. So much for their sales pitch guaranteeing to keep my stuff cold. At least I have something to drink."

She took a swallow, recapped the bottle, and threw it into her open backpack.

"So, Elizabeth, what are you going to do about Mr. Vincent Price? Are you going to tell him the Falcons are due back October fifth?

Really, how can it hurt? I don't remember the field manual saying anything about not divulging the date someone is to return. The manual was precise about how to handle the cards—where to keep them and to be sure to watch when delivery is to resume.

"Hi, Mr. Fowler. Nice to see you out." She put his mail in the box and moved on.

"So if you weren't going to tell him, why did you bring a fresh note card and envelope with you today? Tell me that, will you?"

"Hi, Mrs. Trent."

Elizabeth was running late. The extra time it took to sort her sacks of mail had put her off schedule. She tried to make up the time with her deliveries, but no matter how fast she stopped, stuffed, and stepped on the gas pedal to get to the next box, she continued to lose ground.

"There is no way I'm going to do any extracurricular activities today. He'll just have to wait for the Falcon's return date until tomorrow."

Elizabeth turned left onto Red Snapper Lane. A police car was parked in the Falcon's driveway, and Detective Armstrong was at the front door. She waved to him and buzzed on by box 8236, concentrating on her next stop. Her body was tense as she tried to finish all her deliveries on schedule.

———

JOE DARTED FROM WINDOW to window. The policeman rang the doorbell twice. Joe saw him step away from the door and head to the back of the house. Just as he let the curtain drop into place, he saw Elizabeth dart up the street.

"Damn. She didn't leave a note in the mailbox. Just as well with this officer nosing around. Thank God I didn't leave my bike outside."

Racing to the kitchen, he could see the officer's shadow on the sunroom's white tile.

He's looking in the window. Shit, he almost saw me. Joe flattened his body against the refrigerator and watched as the shadow receded from the floor.

Chapter 18

———

DETECTIVE ARMSTRONG, CLEAN SHAVEN, his portly stomach pouching out over his black belt, sat in his cubby tapping his pen on the calendar desk pad, as he listened to the phone ring for the fourth time. There wasn't much going on for a Monday morning at the department. Most of the on-duty officers were down in the detention cells getting updated statements from those arrested over the weekend. Some stories were changing now that their lawyers were present.

The office area on the second floor was carved into cubicles; the partitions five-feet high—high enough to afford the officers and detectives some privacy but short enough to stand and chat back and forth about a hot case. The murder in Turtle Grove Estates fell into the hot file.

Looking at the notes pinned to the light-grey wool fabric on the walls, Armstrong sat forward to hang up when someone picked up the phone on the other end.

"Hello. Hello, Mr. Falcon?" Armstrong asked.

"No, this is Mrs. Falcon."

"My name is Detective Armstrong, Detective Dick Armstrong, Port Orange Police Department. Is Mr. Falcon there?"

"No, he just left for Florida as a matter of fact."

"Florida? Is he driving?"

"Yes."

"Does he have a cell phone? I'd like to speak with him."

"Yes, he does. Do you have a pen?"

Armstrong made a note of the number. "Thank you, Mrs. Falcon. Have a pleasant day."

Pushing his glasses up on his nose, Armstrong placed the call to Falcon's cell phone.

"Mona, I can't talk now I'm hitting traffic outside of Boston."

"Sorry, Mr. Falcon, I'm Detective Armstrong, Port Orange Police. I just spoke with your wife. She gave me your cell number. Can we talk or should I call you back after the traffic clears?"

"No, no, now is fine. I just didn't want to talk to my wife. She's forever calling me. You know, asking where I am and to drive carefully. What can I do for you, Detective?"

"I suppose you heard about the hurricane that went through Port Orange a few days ago."

"Yes, that's why I'm heading home, to check if my house sustained any damage."

"Well, I'd like to come by and see you once you get back. When do you think you might arrive?"

"I'm trying to make a quick round trip, so hopefully I'll make it as far as Virginia tomorrow. That should put me in Port Orange sometime late Wednesday afternoon. Why? What's up?"

"I'm afraid I have some bad news. During the height of the hurricane, a body was found floating down the canal, a part of the canal that is directly across the road from your house."

"So, what does that have to do with me?"

"Yes, well, I think you know the woman. A Miss Darling, Linda Darling. I believe she's one of the vice presidents at your financial management company...hello...Mr. Falcon. Are you still there?"

———

"HELLO, MISS STITCHWAY, are you there? This is Detective Armstrong."

"Hi, Detective. Sorry about the noise. When I'm delivering the mail, my window's down. Just a minute, let me put this package in the mailbox. Okay. How are you? Hey, call me Elizabeth."

"I'm fine, Elizabeth. We've identified the body, and I wonder if you have ever heard of her, a Miss Linda Darling?"

"Gosh, I don't think so. No. I'm sure I've never heard that name. Who is she?"

"Well, it's an odd coincidence really. She works, or worked, for Mr. Falcon."

"Whoa, that's freaky. Have you told him yet?"

"Yes, I just got off the phone with him. He's driving down from Maine. Said he'd be here late tomorrow afternoon."

Elizabeth now knew for sure she would leave a note for Mr. Price today with this new piece of information. She stepped on the gas, scooting to the next mailbox. "Anything else I can do for you, Detective?"

"Yes, yes, there is. I know I sound like a broken record, but have you seen or heard anything more from your pen pal?"

Oh dear, I don't want Armstrong to think I'm holding out on him. "As a matter of fact, I was going to call you today. I did see him Sunday. I was over at the Spruce Creek recreation area with Maggie, she's my dog, and we ran into each other."

"That is news. Did he give you his name?"

"Yes. We introduced ourselves. He said his name is Vincent Price. And, guess what else?"

"I couldn't. Tell me."

"He said he was a friend of Mr. Falcon's. He's going to be very happy that Mr. Falcon is coming home. He, Mr. Price that is, wants to rent the house until they come back for the winter or at least for the rest of the summer."

"If they're friends, I wonder why Mr. Price didn't call him in Maine."

"Oh, he said he tried. He thought maybe the Falcons were out of the country, you know, vacationing."

"Hmm. I wonder if Mr. Price knew the deceased...Miss Linda Darling?"

Chapter 19

—

ELIZABETH BUMPED ALONG the dirt road, a small stretch in the middle of her delivery route. "Someday I hope they pave this road. That hurricane sure created some deep potholes. There you go, Mr. Brownhill. Sorry about all the bills. Here's a card from your daughter in Wisconsin. That should put a smile on your face." Elizabeth slapped the door shut on the Brownhill mailbox and moved to the next. After three more stops, she carefully executed a U-turn and made a bee-line to get back onto the pavement.

Billowy-white clouds provided Elizabeth with occasional protection from the blistering sun, but nothing cut the humidity. "Just one more month of this steam bath I hope," she said unscrewing the cap of her second bottle of water. Her white tank top from the Orlando Aquarium, three dolphins silk screened surfacing from the ocean waves, topped a pair of white shorts. She hoped the white fabric would conceal the circles of sweat. Her curls were pulled tight through her white ball cap. She fanned her face with a piece of junk mail—a late-summer sale on outdoor grills.

Elizabeth had decided there was no harm in telling what's-his-name the information that Detective Armstrong had related to her. After all, the detective didn't say not to tell anyone. Coming up on the strip of grass before the canal, she made the turn onto Red Snapper Lane and stopped at 8236. She pulled the envelope from her backpack, retrieved the note inside, and read through it once again before depositing it in the box.

Mr. Price,
The Falcons are scheduled to return to their house on October
5. However, Detective Armstrong, whom I spoke with earlier
today, said that Mr. Falcon was on his way back and should
arrive tomorrow, Wednesday, in the afternoon. Detective
Armstrong also said they had identified the body. She is, or
was Miss Linda Darling, and I guess worked for Mr. Falcon.
The detective asked if I had seen the man who helped me that
awful night. I told him, yes, I had run into you at the park, and
that you said your name was Vincent Price. He chuckled. But I
offered not one single word more.
Sincerely,
Elizabeth

Satisfied there were no misspellings, Elizabeth stuffed the letter back in the envelope and opened the mailbox door. She was surprised to see it contained an envelope and once again it was addressed to her. She looked around but didn't see anyone, not even Mrs. Stedly at the top of the lane. She was up and about after her fall and usually waited outside for her mail. Elizabeth laid her letter inside the box, flipped the door shut, and raised the flag.

"There, Mr. Price. A business letter. Real official."

Her hand flew up to the back of her neck. Is someone watching me? She glanced over at the house. Did that shade just move? Oh well, pretty soon all the shades will be open. Mr. Falcon certainly won't want to stay in a gloomy house. I wonder if he's going to arrange Miss Darling's funeral. He must have known her well, being she worked for him. Detective Armstrong didn't mention whether Mrs. Falcon was returning with her husband.

Elizabeth drove to the Stedly mailbox and dropped in the mail. "Don't run, Mrs. Stedly. I'm glad to see you're home and feeling better. Your mail is in the box. Have a nice day."

"Thank you, dear," Mrs. Stedly called out.

Elizabeth drove on. "Even though Detective Armstrong didn't mention an autopsy I imagine one was performed. After all, the woman was murdered. I'm sure her body won't be released until they're satisfied they have all the evidence. All the forensics. I wonder who killed her? Maybe Mr. Falcon will give the detective a lead. He certainly might know if she had any enemies."

Elizabeth quickly finished her route. She was anxious to read the letter from Vincent. Pumping the gas pedal, she moved on to the last mailbox.

Chapter 20

———

JOE'S HEAD SNAPPED UP. The motor groaned raising the two-car garage door. It was early Wednesday afternoon. *Elizabeth's note stated Falcon was expected to return later in the day. He must have gunned it.* Joe grabbed his duffel bag, tucked his coffee cup in the dishwasher, and walked out the Florida room door. He grabbed the handlebars of his motorcycle and crossed the grass. Not looking back, he steered the bike through the hole in the bushes and roared down the street out of Turtle Grove Estates.

———

FALCON ENTERED THE KITCHEN from the garage and immediately felt the cooler air in the house. Wheeling his suitcase to the master bedroom, he passed the thermostat. "Shit, I could have sworn I set the temp at eighty-five before we left. Look at that, seventy-four. What a waste." He continued down the hall and lifted his suitcase up on the bed. Fishing his cell out of his pants pocket, he flipped open the clamshell on the third ring.

"What do you want, Mona? I just walked in the door."

"Hello, Mr. Falcon," Detective Armstrong said. "Glad you're home. I'm in the neighborhood, so if it's alright with you, I'll stop by." The line went dead.

"The bastard hung up before I could answer. Maybe it's alright, and maybe it isn't. Hell, everyone seems to be giving me orders." Walter pulled open the zipper on his suitcase just as the doorbell rang. "In the neighborhood? He must have been around the corner watching for me."

The doorbell rang a second time.

"Hang on. I'm coming."

Armstrong, a burly 250 pounds, was leaning against the doorjamb when Walter yanked open the door. The detective barely saved himself from a nasty fall.

"I take it you're Detective Armstrong?"

"Yes. Sorry, I almost knocked you over falling in the door like that, Mr., Mr. Falcon?"

"Yah. Follow me to the kitchen. I need a cup of coffee. Even though you're on duty would you care to join me?"

"I'd very much like a cup of coffee, thank you. Black."

Armstrong followed Falcon to the kitchen taking note of the rich green satin drapes and velour

couch. Tall, brushed-chrome lamps with white-silk shades sat on the lacquered ebony end tables. Walter was already pouring water into the automatic coffeemaker when Armstrong sat down at the oval, plate-glass table. The kitchen opened to the sunroom. The room where, a few days before, the detective had peeked into the house.

"So, you said Linda Darling is dead. Murdered," Falcon said.

"Appears so, yes. Shot once in the chest...wrapped in a blanket, dumped in the canal across the street. With the rising waters from the hurricane, the body floated down and hit a mail truck."

"Excuse me, a mail truck? In the canal?"

"A gust of wind from the storm lifted your mail lady's vehicle and dumped it into the ditch. I responded to her 911 call. When I arrived the body, still wrapped in the blanket, of course, was resting on the top edge of the bank. A man, a man we haven't been able to locate, apparently helped Miss Stitchway, that's your mail carrier, by lifting the body partially out of the water."

"A man? Who was he?"

"'His name is Vincent Price. Says he's a friend of yours. He's been trying to reach you to rent your house."

"Rent my house? Where is he now?"

"That's just it. We don't know. So many unanswered questions." Armstrong pulled a handkerchief from his back pocket, mopped his brow. "I was hoping you could help, you know, living across the street from where the body was found, and she being one of your employees. Do you have any thoughts about all of this?"

"Maybe. How long do you surmise her body was in the water?"

"Oh, not long. Sam, Sam Houston, he's the county medical examiner, thinks two or three days, but no more than that."

"Well now, it certainly didn't take him long to extract his revenge."

"Excuse me. His revenge?" Armstrong asked, taking a sip from the mug of coffee Falcon had set before him.

"Joe Rocket. That's what he called himself. His real name is Joseph Rockwell."

"Strange name...Rocket."

"For five years he and I were partners in a hedge fund, along with Miss Darling. Rocket had a real knack for picking stocks, and his client's portfolios rocketed to the top, did better than most of the New York-based funds, hence the name Rocket. He was a cocky son-of-a-bitch."

"My, that does seem to be a little cocky, as you say. What happened?"

Falcon took a long sip of coffee, looking over the brim of his mug at the detective, he plunged on. "Three years ago Linda and I caught him embezzling from his clients and our accounts as well."

"No! What did you do?"

"What any red-blooded American would do. We charged him with embezzlement. It took us over a year, but the judge came down on our side and sentenced him to three years in prison."

"Where is he serving his time?"

"That's what I'm trying to tell you, Detective. He was released several days ago...maybe over a week. I'm not sure exactly when. Time served and good behavior. Knowing how devious he is, he probably came straight to Port Orange, killed Linda, and...come to think of it, I'm probably next on his list. He's just waiting for me to come back from my summer home. Oh, my God, I have to alert my wife. He may be on his way to Maine."

"I can see how you would be alarmed, Mr. Falcon. How long were you planning to stay here, in Port Orange? You mentioned on the phone you were returning to be sure the storm didn't damage your property. I didn't see any fallen trees, or pieces of roof missing. Your house seems to have come through the hurricane unscathed."

"Listen, I just got here when you called. I haven't had time to look around. But you're right. I'd better get back to protect my wife. There are a few business issues I have to attend to, and then I'll be on my way...day after tomorrow more than likely. But I'll call Mona right away."

Armstrong stood up, took a few steps to the counter and deposited his empty mug in the sink.

"You've been most helpful, Mr. Falcon. You have things to do, so I'll be on my way. Do keep in touch, especially if you see this Rocket fellow. No need to show me to the door, I'll just go out your sunroom. Goodbye."

"Goodbye, Detective...and keep me posted on the investigation. Maybe something else will come to mind...something that might help you."

As Armstrong went out the back door, Falcon took his mug to the sink, picked up the detective's mug and opened the dishwasher. He froze. There was a coffee mug on the top rack. He was certain Mona had emptied the racks just before they headed out on their trip north.

Closing the dishwasher, Falcon went to the liquor cabinet for a bottle of scotch. He poured himself a stiff drink. Looking at the bottle, tipping it a little to its side, he saw it was almost empty. He made a note on the refrigerator pad to pick up another bottle tomorrow. He could have sworn it was over half full when he left for Maine.

With his drink in hand, he paced around the house, looking in each room. Everything seemed to be in order.

"Now, Walter, don't go getting paranoid. Calm down and start looking for those papers you tucked away. Wish I could remember where I put them." Falcon scrubbed his head. "Hell, don't worry you'll find them...it's been almost two years. How am I going to handle Linda's death? I'm sure there are busybodies in the office who assumed we were having an affair. With my lousy luck, some gossiper will be more than happy to share that tidbit with that detective."

Draining his glass, Walter went back to the kitchen, poured himself another drink and continued his monologue.

"Armstrong said she was shot. The mail lady found her. She said a man helped her. Well, I'd better hurry up and find those documents. Tomorrow. Too much to think about. I'm tired...all that driving. Too tired to do any more tonight."

Falcon sat down in his favorite black-leather office chair and leaned back. *I'll tell Mona there's a good chance I'll have to stay an extra day,* he thought. The scotch helped to calm his nerves and numb his brain. He leaned forward, picked up the phone and called his wife.

"Mona, I'm back in Port Orange."

"Did a Detective Armstrong reach you on your cell phone?"

"Yes." Annoyed at her question, he brought the glass to his lips and drained the last of his scotch.

"What did he want?"

"He told me that the hurricane had washed up a body—Linda Darling. Mona—"

"Oh, no."

"Come on, Mona, don't pretend you feel bad. This is your husband you're talking to. I always know when you're lying."

"It's just—"

"Stop it, Mona. I only called to tell you it's too late for me to do any work tonight, so I'm going to have to stay an extra day."

"Walter, how dare you tell me you're going to stay longer. It can't be Linda this time. So who is she? Who, Walter? Who?"

"Mona, get a hold of yourself. Tell me something. Have you ever heard of a man by the name of Vincent Price?"

"Don't change the subject, Walter. No. I've never heard of a Vincent Price, except for the actor. Who by the way is dead. What's wrong with you, Walter?"

"I don't know...a little edgy knowing Joe's out of prison, I guess. He's very likely to come after me to try to clear his name. Smitty said he told a fellow inmate that he wanted to kill me for framing him."

"Walter, you never told me you framed him."

Chapter 21

———

ELIZABETH AMBLED INTO the kitchen for dinner.

"What's the matter, pumpkin? Somebody give you bad news on the phone?"

"It...Detective Armstrong called. He wanted to know if I had heard any more from Mr. Price. Dad, he said Vincent was a person of interest in the murder of that woman Linda Darling. He also doesn't think that Vincent Price is his real name."

"Who does he think he is, if not a Mr. Price," Martha asked, as she passed the sliced pot roast to her husband.

"He thinks his real name is Joe Rocket, Joseph Rockwell."

"Lizzy, you told us you didn't believe him when he said his name was Price. Why are you shocked?"

"It's not that I'm shocked about his giving me a false name, it's that Armstrong said he was a person of interest. I can't imagine the man who helped me that afternoon in that dangerous hurricane could be capable of shooting someone...of murder." Elizabeth looked into her father's eyes, searching for a little understanding. Seeing nothing, she gazed down at her plate, moving her carrots around in the gravy. She looked up sharply at her dad again.

"I did a search on the internet. Joe Rockwell is, or was, Walter Falcon's business partner. Falcon and Linda Darling charged him with embezzlement. Rocket was found guilty and sent to prison for three years."

"Well, that solves that. This Mr. Rocket couldn't have killed the woman if he was in prison," Harry said putting a dollop of horseradish on his pot roast.

"But that's it, Dad. He was released from prison a few days before the hurricane hit. I almost missed the article...if I hadn't scrolled down the screen...anyway, he didn't kill her. I'm sure of it."

"Well, Elizabeth you certainly are a puzzle," Martha said.

"Why do you say that?" Elizabeth asked, looking up at her mom.

"It's the first time I can recall you have ever come to the defense of someone of the opposite sex, except for your father, of course, and that man you dated in college. Darn, I always forget his name."

"Art. Arthur Knowles."

"Yes, that was it," Martha said. "Harry, have some more broccoli."

"You thought a lot of Art, as I recall," Harry said, scooping another helping of broccoli heads onto his plate. "In fact, your mother and I thought maybe we might be hearing wedding bells."

"Art was using me."

"Elizabeth, what a thing to say," Martha said.

"Lizzy, whatever do you mean?"

"Oh, Dad, it was complicated, that's why I never said anything to you and mom. Art never wanted to go out alone. We were always with another couple...and then just one other couple."

"I don't see how that adds up to using you. Pass the butter please, Harry dear," Martha said splitting her roll open.

"He was checking out our friends' dates, and when he found the one he liked, he tried to make her jealous by being sweet to me."

"Lizzy, he was always very attentive to you whenever we saw you two together."

"Dad, please pass the wine bottle."

"Here, give me your glass. I'll pour it for you."

"It worked."

"What worked?" Martha said looking at her daughter.

"He got the girl. Art told me he had found the girl of his dreams, a beautiful woman, and he was going to marry her. He packed up his possessions, which weren't many because he only stayed in my apartment three months and three days, and said goodbye to me."

"Elizabeth, as I remember you told us you decided the relationship wasn't working out."

"Well, it didn't work out. He was like all the boys in school—wanting me to help with their school assignments—using me. A bunch of bullies."

"Elizabeth, whatever are you saying? What boys in school?"

"All those bullies. Girls, too."

"Lizzy, what bullies? What happened in school...are you talking about the classes you took at the university, or before?"

"The university and before...high school...lots of times."

"Go on, sweetheart, tell us what kind of bullying?" Her father reached across the table and patted her hand, urging her to continue.

"In my freshman year at high school, a group of boys would be waiting outside, taunting me. They said that I'd never have to worry about getting a date...because no boy would ask me out. They said I wasn't pretty with all those red curly kinks in my hair and the buck teeth, and then, of course, the acne."

"You did have a terrible case of acne, but they should never have told you to your face."

"Martha, how can you say such a thing to our daughter?"

"Well, I didn't mean to upset her. It must have been awful."

"Lizzy, honey, you've grown into a beautiful woman. You can't let some old remarks by stupid adolescents hurt you like this...and to carry the memory of them to this day still." Her father picked up the wine bottle and topped off their glasses. "You should have told us. We could have helped you."

"I loved Art. At least I thought I did and I believed he loved me. When he left...that's when I dropped my studies at the university and started to work for the post office. Once I had my own route, I didn't care anymore what guys thought. Most of my clients are happy to see me. They seem to like me."

Elizabeth picked up her glass, took a sip, and wiped her eyes with the back of her hand, and then with her napkin. "It never stopped...a boy, or a man, someone putting me down, Dad. When I talked to the

Chief of Police the year I started college, about a position on the force, he almost laughed...went on and on how difficult the tests were and all the classes I would have to attend."

"Elizabeth, he was just being honest about the work that was involved. I'm sure it wasn't directed at you personally," Martha said.

"I'm sure he thought I wasn't smart enough to be a detective. And, then there is Mr. Perkins. He's always very dismissive of any of my ideas on how we could operate more efficiently. He acts annoyed like I'm bothering him."

"Now, Lizzy, I've met Mr. Perkins. He's told me how hard you work, and that you're one of his most valuable carriers. When you went full time, he gave you the longest route knowing you could handle it. I had no idea you harbored these self-doubts. You're always so in command of yourself. Always planning your days. You absolutely can be whatever you want to be."

"Of course I can do it. I feel like I can do just about anything I want. If I want to be a private investigator, I know I can. In fact, I'm taking some online courses for investigative procedures, and forensic science."

Martha and Harry exchanged looks of concern.

"Your mother and I didn't know you were so actively pursuing your dream of being an investigator. You know what I think?"

"What?" Elizabeth asked, blowing her nose. She sat back down at the table and sipped the last of her wine.

"Martha, put on a pot of coffee, please. We're going to have a serious discussion with our daughter about her future."

"Dad, I'm okay...really."

"No, you're not. I want you to exorcize these notions. Do you hear me? Lizzy, any woman who can get all dolled up in bright colors like you do, must have an abundance of self-worth inside, a very positive outlook on life that you're not recognizing in yourself. Then there's your curiosity, persistence, determination and your awareness of your surroundings, not to mention your photographic memory."

"Thanks, Dad, but I think you're just a bit prejudice."

"You wanted to enter law enforcement, and you let some stupid police chief tell you it was too hard. So what. Nothing that you really want is going to be easy."

"I know that, but—"

"No buts about it. Did you or did you not score the highest ever on the tests you had to take even to be considered as a mail carrier?"

"I did."

"Ah, a smile. That's more like it. Lizzy, you just remember all those traits I ticked off. Sounds like a resume for a private investigator to me."

"Here's your coffee you two and a piece of your favorite triple-layer chocolate cake, Harry."

"I swear if that therapist doesn't get me walking soon, I'll be three-hundred pounds," Harry said digging into his cake. "My limbs won't be able to hold me up. Now, Lizzy, I think this Mr. Price can help both of you. You believe him. That's the first step. And, don't forget we have evidence that he was there, the mud from that shoe. He wasn't a figment of your imagination."

"Oh, Dad, I don't see how that will help. But, I do have a plan."

"That's better. Let's hear it."

"Remember a few days ago I called to let you and mom know I was going to be late for dinner?"

"Yes, I remember," Harry said taking a bite of cake.

"Well, I was on a case."

"A case?" Harry said, stopping his fork midway to his mouth.

"Yes, I've been doing some part-time work for Goodwurthy Private Investigators."

"I've heard of them," Harry said. "Honestly, Lizzy, you never cease to amaze me. Go on. Go on."

"Oliver Goodwurthy, he started the company, was in a jam a while ago. Too much business. He placed a small ad in the Pennysaver news sheet. He needed help, and the main qualification was knowing how to search the internet for information. So, I went to see him, and he hired me on a trial basis."

"Seems like you've been holding out on us on several issues," Martha said.

"I know, Mom, and I'm sorry. I was going to tell you several times, but at first, I didn't think it would lead anywhere but after this last case...well, maybe it will."

"What did you do...for this case?" Harry asked.

"Actually it was straightforward. Oliver, he asked me to call him that, was in Atlanta and needed to find a missing person who loved the Daytona Beach biker events. Seems she and her fiancé went missing just before a big wedding. I lucked out really. When I did a search, and the first thing in the list was an ad for biker weddings, I called and pretended I was the woman's friend and was frantic to find her as I was supposed to be at the wedding."

"And did the person know of this woman?" Martha asked.

"Mom, it was wonderful. Yes, she did and told me when and where the ceremony was going to take place."

"And you went?" Harry asked. "That's why I was late for dinner. I took pictures for them. I called Oliver to let him know I found them and where they were staying. It was fun, easy, and so satisfying. You know, I'm not sure why I was so depressed when we started dinner. I guess I couldn't believe that the mystery man could be a murderer. I should have confided in you both sooner."

"Let that be a lesson, young lady," Harry said with a twinkle in his eye. "Your mother and I are on your side, you know."

"I know, Dad. There's the phone. I'll get it. Hello. Hello." Elizabeth looked at the phone and then returned the receiver to the hook.

"Who was that, Lizzy?"

"Wrong number I guess. The line went dead."

"Elizabeth, you said Mr. Price left you a letter today. What did he have to say?" Martha asked topping off her husband's coffee cup.

"Nothing new. All he did was ask me again if I knew when the Falcons were coming home and was there any more information on the body. Questions I had already answered in the note I put in the mailbox today. But, you know what, I'm going to keep my eyes open just in case I come across something. After all, the body floated up into the bumper of my vehicle, so I'm kind of involved. Don't you think?"

"Damn right, you're involved. And then this Mr. Price, or Rocket, or whatever his name is, is leaving notes for you in that mailbox," her dad said leaning forward.

"8236," Elizabeth said, her ruby lips parting in a big smile.

Chapter 22

———

THE LOCKSMITH REPLACED THE mechanism on the front door and was now working on the sunroom entrance. Falcon leaned against the wall watching the man remove the old lock. He took another sip of his coffee.

"Okay, Joe, come and get me," he whispered.

"Sorry, Mr. Falcon. Did you say something?"

"No, no. Just thinking out loud."

"I'm almost done here...then I'll be out of your hair."

Falcon topped off his coffee. He was planning his search, the locations, which to tackle first.

Within minutes he heard the locksmith pack up his tools. He paid the man and in return was handed two new sets of keys to the house.

Falcon pocketed the keys and started his dissection of the house looking for incriminating records—deposits into a secret bank account in Mexico. He had a pretty good idea where he had stashed the documents three years ago—in the office. Now sweating from the hot coffee and too many clothes, he first went into the bedroom to change into his tan shorts and white tank top. He sat on the edge of the bed and stepped into his flip-flops, lying on the floor where he had kicked them off last night. Sniffing the air, he closed his eyes a moment. "Umm, Linda's perfume, or maybe its Mona's. Nice."

Anxious to ease his mind that he had taken care of the damning papers, he strode through the living room to the office. Pausing in the doorway, he gazed fondly at the ceiling-high cherry bookcases on either side of the picture window and continued along the wall on the left side. "Rocket, you did a masterful job designing this space. Too bad you had to leave it so suddenly."

Falcon opened the top drawer of the four-drawer cherry file cabinet. He knew Joe had it built to his specification out of the same wood as the bookcases. Caressing the finely polished surface, he remembered the shock on Joe's face when he learned that his partner was calling for payment on the note to his house. Walter could still hear Joe whining: "You want me to pay off the note? Walter, you know I can't. My lawyer says he needs more time to prepare the case. I have no funds. You know everything of mine is tied up in our business. You have to let me clear myself, get back in sync with the market."

Poor Joe. He never saw it coming. Falcon glanced around the room, now his office in his house. "It was a brilliant idea if I do say so myself. Offering to loan him money with his house as collateral. What a shame his attorney charged such high fees to defend him."

Walter looked out the window at a stand of small palm trees. "But, Joe, it was your own fault. You always had to hire the best, always putting on a front to your clients that they were in good hands."

Chuckling, Falcon could still see the hatred in Linda's eyes when she realized she wasn't getting anywhere with Joe when he continually rebuffed her advances. "She was such an easy mark. She jumped at my suggestion to hurt you, Mr. Rocket, to hurt you where it would cause you the most pain—charges of embezzling money from your precious clients, ruining your pristine reputation. Ahh, such great memories."

Falcon left the file drawer open and eased himself into the black-leather lounger. He gently pushed the button raising the footrest in one smooth electronic motion. His eyes fixated on the picture in the gold frame sitting to the side on the carved cherry desk. A picture of the three of them—himself, Joe, and Linda. "Oh, my friends, those were the days, the three of us smiling. You were both suckers. Neither one of you could see it coming. Now, here I am reaping and enjoying the fruits of your labors. Joe, you should have stopped. What's that phrase—stop and smell the roses? Yes, that's it. All you wanted to do was work, work, work. Money, money, money—there was never enough for you. No portfolio ever grew fast enough. No time for women or maybe you thought no woman was worth your time. Who knows, my friend, if you had shown even the slightest interest in Linda, my scheme might not have succeeded."

Falcon pushed the second button on the chair's remote control and the footrest lowered. He stood, took a step, and picked up the gold frame. "Linda, my beautiful Linda. So many wonderful interludes in my bed while poor Mona withered away in Maine. Thank you again for your help."

Roughly replacing the picture on the desk, Falcon retreated to the kitchen to refresh his coffee. "Come on Walter, now is not the time to meander down memory lane. There will be plenty of opportunities to savor your victory over Mr. Joseph Rockwell." Falcon retraced his steps to the office and the open file cabinet. *Better find those deposit tickets, and, oh yes, the monthly reports for the two, or was it three years you transferred funds from Joe's clients to my own?*

Not finding what he was looking for in the first drawer, his fingers skimmed the tabs of the folders in the second and third drawers. Without stopping to open the fourth, he slapped the side of his head, stood up, and walked briskly to the bookcase to the left of the window. "Dummy, how could you forget where you put the papers? Well, it has been several years," he said answering himself.

"Here you are." A grin spread over his face. He sat on the floor cross-legged and reached for a set of four books from the bottom shelf. Pulling them out of the bookcase, it was evident the four spines were fake, revealing a single box. "I remember buying you in a bookstore." He fondly ran his hands over the fake books. He laid the box on the carpet in front of him and opened the cover. It was filled with several tubes of rolled-up sheets of paper.

Chuckling, he closed the case, and with the fake books in hand headed to the garage. "I know just where I'm going to put you."

In the garage, he laid the box on the workbench and pressed the garage door opener mounted on the wall. He backed the car out a few feet and returned to the workbench. He continued to chuckle thinking that if Rocket came calling again, he, Walter Falcon, could blackmail him for good with the cards he didn't play the first time. He'd make it look like Linda helped Joe to embezzle the money. "You bastard." *Too bad Linda's dead but lucky for me because she can't turn against me. She can't reverse her story to help you. Once I let you in on that little secret, you won't dare bother me again.*

Falcon pulled down the attic stairs from the garage ceiling, climbed up into the crawl space, and tucked the box behind some ceiling rafters—just a small stack of four books. He climbed back down the wooden stairs, pulled the rope raising the ladder into the ceiling and returned to the kitchen to call Mona.

"Hi, my dear Mona. You'll be happy to hear I'm done with my business and I'm heading back to Maine. Put one of those bottles of champagne from the wine cabinet into the refrigerator to chill. We'll have ourselves a little celebration. I'm sure you'll enjoy that."

Falcon finished his conversation with his wife, dumped the cold coffee grounds down the disposal, and put his coffee cup in the dishwasher. He looked down at the other cups in the top rack. "Ah, my dear friend, no more drinking my coffee. Your key won't open the doors anymore. All you can do now is look in the window with a sorry face seeing what was once yours but will never be again."

Grabbing his suitcase, he returned to the garage. Throwing the case in the trunk, he climbed into his car and headed out of Turtle Grove Estates.

———

JOE WATCHED FALCON back out of the driveway. Once he was out of sight, Joe entered the house through an unlatched sunroom window, shaded by a large holly bush.

Chapter 23

——

JOE CHECKED THE DISHWASHER. It was partially filled with dirty dishes from the day-and-a-half Falcon was home. The cup Joe had used was untouched, remaining on the top rack.

"Well, partner, did you realize I was staying in your house? Rather, my house? Of course, you did, why else would you have changed the locks? You certainly made a quick trip. I wonder why? Could it have been you heard I was released from prison?"

Joe headed to the office still mulling over the possible reasons for Falcon's hasty trip. "Was it to check for downed palm trees as you told Detective Armstrong? I think not. My bet is you were looking for something that might incriminate you and clear me, and given your short visit you probably found what you were looking for."

Even though it was less than an hour since Falcon pulled out of the driveway, the temperature and humidity were building in the house. Joe walked down the hall to the thermostat and shifted the setting down to seventy-six and then continued on down the hall.

He stood in the doorway to the office and slowly scanned every object from one wall to the next, to the next and finally the last. Then the tables tops, the desk, and—. "You moved the picture of you and Linda, and I...there's a dust mark. You didn't put it back exactly where it was. Okay, let's look for more disturbed dust."

Joe started at one end of the room, now looking closer at each surface for more marks indicating that something had been moved. Slowly shuffling a few feet at a time, scanning floor to ceiling at whatever was in front of him, he continued to move around to the left-side of the window.

"Damn. Seems you didn't move anything except that picture." Shuffling the last two feet and now standing at the far end of the bookcase, he checked the base of each shelf. Seeing nothing, he turned away to look once again at the desk.

"Wait a minute." He spun around, back to the bookcase. "Here's a clean space—no dust. Walter, my boy, you removed a large book...and it appears you didn't put it back. Now, the question is, did you take it with you or did you put it in a better hiding place?"

With his hands on his hips, Joe again slowly shuffled along all the shelves. He didn't know what he was looking for, but he was certain he'd know it if he saw it. Nothing shouted out, "over here." He sat in the black-leather recliner. Not bothering with the footrest, he leaned forward scanning the room again.

Not seeing any more dust lines, Joe headed back to the kitchen. "If I wanted to hide something in this house, where would I put it?" Absentmindedly, he fixed a small pot of coffee. His mind skipped along to the gurgle of the percolating coffeemaker visualizing each room—floor to ceiling. The gurgling stopped. He retrieved his cup from the dishwasher, filled it with the fresh brew, and sat down at the kitchen table, completing his mental trip around the house. Jumping up from the table, spilling his coffee as he banged the cup down on the kitchen counter, he headed for the garage.

"I knew it, you son-of-a-bitch. You made it too easy for me. The attic stairs never did return flush with the ceiling unless you tease it a little. Let's see if you left your dear friend a present."

Joe pulled the cord lowering the wooden ladder. Carefully looking at each board before he stepped on it, watching for a sign that Walter had been there, he climbed until his shoulders were an inch above the floor of the crawl space. "The dust is certainly my keeper today. I can see every step you took, first to the right, no, no, you circled back to the left, shuffled around, and now back to the stairs."

Joe continued his forward movement to the top step and slowly made his way to the rafters where it appeared that the dust had been kicked around. Not seeing anything out of the ordinary, he slowly moved around in the cleaned spot an inch at a time, and then he saw it.

"Lookie here. Books. Uh, no, a box that looks like several books." Picking up the box he returned to the top of the stairs and sat down to see what was inside. The light was too dim, so he climbed down the ladder, pulled the cord to raise the wooden staircase, then tugged again, so it slipped into its proper place in the ceiling. He left the garage and headed to the kitchen where the light was better.

At the kitchen table, he opened the box and removed four large rolls of paper. The first roll, made him shudder. "Linda, how could you have done this? You withdrew thousands of dollars from Mr. Thompson's account...and here...fifty grand." Joe examined more of the documents, a sick feeling creeping into his stomach. Another roll showed transfers from her account to Falcon's. The last roll had bank statements covering a period of almost twenty-four months with money deposited at the end of each month.

Tilting back in the tan-leather kitchen chair, Joe knew he was looking at evidence that could turn the tables on Linda and Walter. But with Linda dead, Falcon could pin everything on her leaving himself in the clear. Joe couldn't let that happen because the embezzlement charges against him would not be nullified. He would be barred from doing the one thing he did best, the one thing he loved—buying and selling stock for his clients, building the wealth of all their portfolios.

"I have to see Elizabeth. I need her help." Looking at his watch, Joe knew he had to hurry. It was almost time for her to drive by. Darting back to the office, he sat behind the desk, pulled a piece of paper from the printer, an envelope out of the second drawer, and scribbled a note. Leaving the house by way of the sunroom, making sure he left it unlocked, he glanced up and down the street. No one was in sight. Cutting through the bushes to the main road, he casually walked to the corner of Red Snapper Lane and turned to walk up the street. He stopped in front of the mailbox, put in his letter, raised the flag, and retraced his steps back to the house.

Once back in the house, he carefully bundled the rolls of paper back into the box and returned it to its hiding place. He then went to the living room to watch out a slit in the blinds to be sure Elizabeth picked up the note.

Joe heaved a sigh of relief when she rounded the corner. He saw her stop at the mailbox, and with his letter in her hand, she pushed the flag down just as a squad car pulled up behind her.

———

"GOOD AFTERNOON, ELIZABETH," Detective Armstrong called out.

"Hi, Detective. If I didn't know better I'd say you were following me," she said with a laugh.

"No, no. I thought I'd ask Mr. Falcon a few more questions. Have a nice day."

"You, too. Bye." Setting the letter she had just removed from the seat beside her, she stepped on the gas and rolled to her next mailbox.

Detective Armstrong sauntered up to the front door and rang the bell. He waited standing on one foot and then the other. He rang the bell again. Giving up he returned to his squad car and drove off, waving to Elizabeth as he drove by her.

Elizabeth had to admit that when she spotted the flag up on 8236, she felt a slight flutter in her stomach. However, by the time she pulled down the door to the box she was in total control. After all, Mr. Falcon could have left some mail he wanted her to pick up. But, when she saw the note was addressed to 'Elizabeth' and recognizing Vincent's handwriting, and then seeing the detective walk up to the Falcon front door, she became very flustered, her heart raced a bit, and she felt tongue-tied.

Chastising herself for being a silly school girl, she drove on depositing mail in a few more boxes. After the detective drove by and waved, her curiosity got the better of her. She pulled away from the last box and drove to a group of bushes along a pond. She slit open the envelope being careful not to get a paper cut. Opening the triple-folded piece of paper she read the short note, fanning herself with the envelope.

> Dear Elizabeth,
> Thank you for the information that the body has been identified and that the Falcons are due back in October. It was also beneficial to know that Mr. Falcon was driving back to Port Orange. I did see him.
> Elizabeth, I want to offer you a business proposition in your capacity as a PI. Can you
> come to the house this evening, seven o'clock? I would appreciate it if you would give me a chance to explain a few things. It would be best if no one saw you. There is a hole in the bushes directly across from the canal. I'll leave the sunroom door ajar. Bring Maggie if you like.
> If you decide not to come, I'll understand you don't want to get involved. In which case, thank you for your last note.
> Sincerely,
> Vincent

Chapter 24

——

THE OVERWHELMING FORCE driving Joe was to punish Falcon, watch him squirm, see terror in his eyes as he came to the realization he was going to lose everything, maybe even his life. Joe paced around the kitchen, up and down the hall, and out to the sunroom, pondering the best way to extract his revenge on Falcon, the man who had ruined his reputation, stolen his money, and bilked his clients out of thousands of their dollars. Joe also had a feeling that Falcon was responsible for Linda's death. He didn't care about Linda. He didn't care about any woman. Never had. His ambition was to fill his coffers as well as those of his clients, but always within the law. If he could prove Falcon murdered Linda, his revenge would be that much sweeter.

He needed evidence. Once he had proof of Falcon's crimes then, and only then, would he go to the police. Without evidence showing beyond a reasonable doubt that Falcon murdered Linda, the courts might only give Falcon a few years, plus order him to pay restitution to Joe for his wrongful imprisonment. But murder in a death-penalty state, ah, that would be worth paying for a ringside seat to watch him take his last breath.

It was almost seven o'clock. Joe sat in the sunroom watching the hole in the bushes where he told Elizabeth to enter the yard.

——

THE BRIGHT NEON LIGHTS of the ice cream parlor danced around the building on the corner of Central Park and Spruce Creek Road. Families were queued up at the outside window, kids laughing and tugging on the arms of their parents waiting for their treats. The air had cooled from the heat of the day. The gaily striped umbrella tables—yellow, blue, red, and green—were all occupied. Friends, families, and lovers coming to life over a dish of ice cream, relieved to escape the oppressive high temperature once again. Escape at least until the morning sun restored the heat wave.

Elizabeth parked her car in a spot on the outer fringe of the parlor's parking lot. Grabbing Maggie's leash, she set off down the street to Turtle Grove Estates for her meeting with Mr. Price.

Twenty minutes later she and Maggie disappeared from the sidewalk as they scooted through a hole in the bushes to the back door of 8236. Elizabeth tapped her knuckles on the door once. The door gave way. *He did say he was going to leave it ajar,* she thought. With a slight nudge, the door opened a little wider. "Vincent. Vincent, are you there?"

"Yah. Come on in, Elizabeth," he said opening the door wide inviting her to step inside. However, seeing Maggie, he stepped out instead. "Ah, Maggie, yes, it's nice to see you, too." He knelt down on the grass, giving the dog a scratch behind both ears. She rolled over so he could give her a tummy rub as well, then jumped up, shook herself, and gently kissed his cheek, her tail wagging.

"She sure seems to like you," Elizabeth said. "Maybe we should just talk out here."

"Elizabeth, I'm not going to hurt you, and besides you have your bodyguard with you. Come on in. The coffee's perking. Come on," he said nodding his head toward the inside.

Elizabeth followed Joe thru the sunroom into the kitchen. It was still light out so she could see where she was walking but darkness would descend within the hour. She stopped at the glass kitchen table, laid her purse down on one of the tan leather chairs. The room was light and airy with a bay window letting in the greenery of the garden. Bushes circled the lawn drawing the boundaries of the property.

"Detective Armstrong talked to me. Wanted to know where you were, or if I'd seen you. He thinks your name is Joe Rocket, which is just about as bad as Vincent Price."

"He's right, Elizabeth. That's one thing I wanted to tell you tonight. I'm sorry I lied to you. I didn't want to get you involved except for finding out when the Falcon's were returning for the winter."

Elizabeth's eyes popped at his admission.

"I know you take cream in your coffee, but I only have sugar."

"Black is fine." Elizabeth looked around and began to relax in the cozy yet sophisticated kitchen—white walls and cabinets with black granite counters. Snapping back to why she had dared to meet with this man, she said, "Now let's get to it, Vincent, err, Joe. Are you friends of the Falcons? And what's this about a business proposition?"

Joe laid out two red cotton placements on the table and then handed Elizabeth a black coffee mug with the company name: "Falcon, Darling, and Rockwell, Investment Advisers," printed in gold letters. She picked it up, took a sip, then put the cup down on the placemat. He sat in a chair opposite her sipping his coffee.

"I told you I was a stockbroker. What I didn't tell you is that Walter Falcon and Linda Darling were my partners."

"Really? Were you and she, you know, an item?"

"No. I had no personal life. Never wanted to get involved in a relationship, and certainly not with a woman like Linda. She was very conniving."

"By the way, how did you get into this house?" Elizabeth asked. Her brown eyes never left his face.

"After I helped you out of the canal, I used my own key. Falcon changed the locks before he left yesterday morning."

"You had a key to this house? You must be a very good friend. But wait a minute, how did you get in today?"

"Just in case he did change the locks, I unlatched the window at the end of the sunroom before he arrived. By the way, thanks for alerting me that Falcon was on his way back here."

"I don't get it if you're friends—"

"This is my house or was before Falcon conned me out of it. He stupidly never changed the locks, so my key fit, that is until yesterday."

"Oh, Joe that's awful. But a man as smart as you...how did you let that happen?"

"Unbeknownst to me, Falcon, and now I find that Linda was in on it too, embezzled money from my client's and my personal account. Then he accused me of stealing the funds, as well as money from the company, and turned me into the police."

"But you must have had a lawyer. A good lawyer would be able to clear you wouldn't he?"

"I thought so, but Falcon was very diligent in covering his tracks. All the evidence of the missing funds pointed to me. Falcon cleaned me out."

"I had no idea he was such a devious person. The Falcons left me a generous twenty dollar bill in the mailbox at Christmas time."

Joe leaned forward and looked intently into Elizabeth's eyes. "I told you I was sorry I lied to you. If I'm going to ask for your assistance, I have to trust you with the whole story." Joe sighed, took a sip of coffee and looked back at Elizabeth. He was putting his life in a woman's hands. This was a first for him, and he feared he might be making a mistake. But he needed information, and he felt she could find it for him.

"When I entered the house, the night of the hurricane, I checked the safe I had installed in the office at the time I built this place. Falcon knew about the safe, and in fact, I had to give him the combination as part of a court order when he took possession of my property. I was hoping he kept some cash in it as I had done."

"Well, did he? Was there money in the safe?"

"I'm happy to say he did and I took it. All of it."

"Oh, dear. That sounds like stealing. I'm not sure you should have told me that." Elizabeth's eyes sparkled, and a smile crossed her face. "On the other hand, it serves him right for what he did to you."

Joe took her smile as a sign of acceptance and plunged on. "That's what I've been living on since I was released."

"Released?"

"Stitch, I spent the last year-and-a-half in prison, the Apalachee Correctional Institution near Tallahassee."

"When did you get out...of prison?"

"Three days before the hurricane. I hopped a freight train...I had very little money...only a few bucks. The train used to stop on the north side of the river, but while I was away, I guess they changed procedures. It slowed down a little but didn't stop. I jumped into the river."

"Joe, you could have killed yourself. That was a crazy thing to do."

"I know, but I made it, fought the current, and swam to the dock. My plan was to get into the house, find my money or his money, and of course, start to execute my plan to get back at Falcon. What I hadn't planned on was the hurricane. I saw you get blown into the canal. That's when I rushed over to help you."

"Thanks again for that. It was one scary night."

"Has Detective Armstrong said anything more about Linda Darling? Any leads as to her killer?"

"No, except that he says you are a person of interest. Did you kill Linda? I mean this is a pretty wild story you've just told me." Elizabeth pulled Maggie's leash, so the dog was closer. "You think Mr. Falcon may have killed her, but for all, I know she was first on your hit list. You could have killed her and made it look like Mr. Falcon did it."

"For God's sake, Elizabeth, you have to believe me."

When Joe raised his voice, Maggie stood up and moved even closer to Elizabeth. "It's okay, girl," she said caressing the dog's silky head. "Joe, or whoever you are, I think I'd better leave."

Elizabeth stood up, slinging her tote over her shoulder. Joe stood at the same time.

"Look. You check with the Apalachee prison. They'll tell you I was released and when. Released for good behavior mind you. If the police think the man who helped you is Joe Rocket, then it won't be long before they learn that I owned this house. And, if they look at the trial transcripts, they'll find that I threatened Falcon the day I was sentenced. Handcuffs and two officers restrained me. I was mad as hell, and scared, and wanted to get my hands on the bastard. The police may even check this house from time to time, to see if I return."

"Maybe that's what the detective was doing today when he stopped. I noticed he went to the front door, but when nobody answered, he looked around and then drove away."

"I know. I was here. Falcon had left a couple hours earlier to return to Maine. Look, I bought a cell phone. Let me give you the number. Do you have a cell?"

"Yes, but, I don't know about talking to you."

"You think over what I've said. Check it out. I need your help."

"Okay, but I warn you, I'll have to tell Armstrong at some point." Elizabeth wrote her cell number on the paper napkin and shoved it over to Joe at the same time picking up the napkin with his number.

"I'm leaving the house tonight," he said. "I can't come back here. I'll be picked up for sure. However, you, you go by here every day, but no more notes in the mailbox."

"You still haven't told me about your business proposition."

"I need to prove that Falcon framed me and most important that he murdered Linda. You said you were going to open up shop as a private eye. I want to hire you as my investigator."

"Your investigator? A PI as in private investigator?"

"Yes, will you do it?"

"Oh, my." Elizabeth strode into the sunroom, head down in concentration, paced around the furniture. Maggie followed her then sat in the middle of the floor, waiting for her mistress to stop going around in circles. *Now, what do you do?* She thought to herself. *Can you trust him? On the other hand, if it turns out he's lying, I'll turn him into Armstrong quicker than a blink of my eye. My own case. Why not?*

Elizabeth marched back into the kitchen, hands on her hips. She stood in front of Joe who was waiting for her, putting their cups in the dishwasher, marking time.

"Okay, I'll do it. But there's a matter of my fee."

"Your fee. Of course, I'm going to pay you."

"PIs get a retainer, money to start investigating...for expenses."

"That's fair."

"If you want me to begin investigations into this matter, my retainer, which must be paid up front, is $2000. I charge an hourly rate of $100, which means my first twenty—"

"I know, your first twenty hours are deducted from the retainer, and—"

"That's correct. You will be billed for any additional time over the first twenty hours plus expenses, of course."

"Of course. I—"

Maggie jumped up growling as the back door swung open.

"Well now, isn't this sweet. Joey, I wasn't sure who this mail dolly was talking to, so I decided to check her out."

"Shit, Gus, put that gun away."

"Joey, honestly, I didn't know it was you. I guess Falcon's gone, huh, or did you already do away with him?"

"No, I didn't do away with him. Now get out of here."

"Aren't you going to introduce your pal Gus to your girlfriend?"

Elizabeth moved back as the men talked. She kept a strong hold on the leash, pulling Maggie to the far side of the kitchen away from the stranger. Maggie reluctantly moved but kept her fangs bared. A low guttural growl rolled around in her throat.

"She's not my girlfriend, and I told you I don't need your help."

"Okay, okay. I was in the neighborhood, you know, watching out for you, keeping you outta trouble like old times. I see this dolly sneaking in through the back, and I figured I should check her out."

"Alright, you've checked her out."

"Yeah, well, I'll be going then. See you around, dolly." Gus stuffed the gun in his pocket and once again disappeared out the back door.

Maggie stopped growling and sat down beside Elizabeth, leaning into her leg.

"Who was that?"

"A guy."

"Obviously, but what did he mean when he said he was watching out for you like old times?"

"We were inmates together. He protected me from some pretty mean characters when we were out in the yard. I'm sorry he barged in like that. He has some strange idea that I still need his protection."

"I see. Do you...still, need his help?"

"No. I need your help."

"Come on, Maggie, we have work to do."

Chapter 25

——

"HEY, LIZZY. Cat got your tongue?"

"What? Oh, Helen. Hi?"

"Where's your head, girl? Looks like we have a light load today, no circulars. See you later."

"Good morning, Elizabeth. Everything going well on your route?"

"Yes, sir. Everything's business as usual. Thanks for asking." Mr. Perkins walked on by and Elizabeth, finished with her sorting, pushed her bin out to the yard and packed her vehicle. She threw her lime-green tote onto the floor by her side. The tote matched her shorts, topped with a white-T-shirt stenciled with pink flamingos, pink sequins dotting their eyes. The humidity was still oppressive, but her lime-green ball cap kept the curls off her neck after she pulled them as a bunch through the cap's hole.

On her way to the first mailbox, her mind wandered back to Joe's request the night before. PI! "OK, Sherlock, what would a PI do at this moment? Well, not this moment, but when I'm done with the mail for today...go see the coroner," she said, slapping the wheel as she skirted a Votran bus. "He just might give me some useful information. I can say I was in the neighborhood, and...and ask if anyone has claimed the body? That's it."

Armed with a game plan, Elizabeth's spirits rose, a smile crossed her face, her eyes grew bright in anticipation. *I'm on the job!*

"Hi, Mr. Fowler. Looks like Sam's after that squirrel. She's pulling you at a fast trot."

"Hi, Lizzy. That she is."

Laughing, Elizabeth scooted up the next road, and one by one opened the mailbox doors with a flourish, tossed the mail inside, flipped up the door and moved on, humming as she did so. "Helen was right. I'll be finished early and then, Mr. Sam Houston, I hope you're prepared for a visit from the newest PI in Port Orange."

———

PI STITCHWAY WALKED WITH a spring in her step down the gray, concrete-block hallway of the building that housed the morgue, quelling the urge to skip to her first questioning assignment. The air was chilly, and she made a note to herself to bring a sweater if she came here again. Stepping into the coroner's office, she was again hit with the strong odor of chlorine.

"Miss Stitchway, I believe, if my memory is intact." He rose shaking her hand.

"Yes, Mr. Houston." Elizabeth answered smiling. She sat in the visitor's chair next to his desk.

"What brings a nice young lady to see this old man?"

"I would not call you an old man. I was just in the neighborhood and thought I'd drop in to see if anyone had claimed that body I found? I pass the spot every day, you know, so I'm constantly reminded of the sight of that arm hanging out of the blanket."

"Yes, that would be quite a shock, indeed."

Elizabeth stood up, walked over to three gray two-drawer file cabinets. Hanging on the wall above the cabinets were several diplomas. Scattered around the diplomas were pictures of Houston when he was younger. Several others showed his chronological journey through the years—pictures with various dignitaries in the Daytona Beach area.

"Mr., oops, I see from the diploma here that you're a doctor. Please excuse me for not addressing you properly. That must have taken a long time and a lot of work."

"Quite so. My work has turned out to be very interesting, especially with all the new technology. Journals advising me of this and that hit my in-box every day. DNA is giving us so much information, irrefutable evidence in many cases."

Returning to another chair across from the coroner, Elizabeth leaned back. "That was quite a heavy blanket she was wrapped in. The body. Even soaked with the rain, it looked to have a pattern, many colors as I remember."

"That's right. You're very observant, my dear. The blanket is Turkish in origin. Quite beautiful...a tapestry weave."

"I sure can smell the chlorine in your office. Does it make you want to sneeze all the time?"

"No, no. When I open the door to the laboratory, the rush of air brings along the odor. The lab must be kept absolutely spotless, disinfected, because of the autopsies."

"I don't know how you do it. Was the bullet still in her body? It must have been a big one to kill her. You said she was shot once in the chest...the day Detective Armstrong asked me to see you. You know, he was wondering if I recognized her."

"Oh my, no. It was a .38 caliber...large enough to kill her but small enough, and entering with such velocity, it went clear through her body."

"Where are you from, doctor...you sound very English."

"Australia, my dear. A long way from home. But you didn't wander in here to talk about me. You asked if anyone had come forth to claim the body. Her brother reported her missing a day or two after the storm. Detective Armstrong took the call and, from the brother's description suggested the two of them meet here at the morgue. The detective told him that a Jane Doe had been found and that the body was still unidentified."

"So, her brother identified Miss Darling? Seeing her like that, all messed up, must have been an awful shock. What's his name, Brother Darling?"

"Brother Darling goes by the moniker of Timothy. So the detective told you her name?"

"Oh, yes. He's asked me to help him with the case, you know, since I found the body, and I'm at the scene daily, except for Sunday."

"Of course. No mail on Sunday." The coroner chuckled. "Mr. Darling was shocked, but you know, Miss Stitchway, I wouldn't say he was upset."

Chapter 26

———

A NOR'EASTER SLAMMED into the New England coastline. Falcon, his body rigid with tension, leaned over the steering wheel straining to see the road in front of him. The wipers swiped back and forth at high speed but were not even close to keeping the windshield clear. Wind buffeted his big black Cadillac. The weatherman's voice screeched from the car's radio alerting anyone listening that the storm was intensifying and warned motorists to stay off the highways.

Sweat poured from Falcon's forehead and armpits. A sudden pain seared his chest. "Oh no, no, not a heart attack. Stop. Get off the road, you idiot."

Seeing an overpass a few yards ahead, he pulled off the highway and stopped the car. Laying his head back on the headrest, he tried to breathe, but the pain was too intense. Reaching into the glove compartment, he fumbled for the vial of pills his doctor had prescribed should chest pains return. Three years ago he had been rushed to the hospital with a mild heart attack. The doctor had warned him to keep the pills near him at all times in case of another episode.

"Okay, doc, you said if I experienced strong pains to take this nitro. It better work." Opening the bottle, he tapped out a pill into his hand. His hand shook, but he managed to get enough strength and steadiness to put the pill under his tongue. Then the remaining coffee spilled on his white golf shirt, down onto his thigh, and puddling on the rubber floor mat.

The windows of the car quickly steamed over. He reached for the keys and turned the engine on so that the air conditioning would run. The steam cleared. Resting with his head leaning back, arms limp at his sides, he began to catch his breath.

His hands now steady, Falcon leaned forward, put the car in gear, and ventured out again into the sheets of pouring rain.

Approaching the bridge connecting New Hampshire to Maine, he slowed to a crawl, passing four police cars with their red lights twirling in the mist. Then he saw them—two cars were in the ditch, one overturned. He drove up the steep incline onto the bridge traversing the Piscataqua River. He gripped the wheel in an effort to keep the car from being blown against

the guardrail. "Come on, Walter, just get over the bridge. You're almost home."

He saw his exit off the highway just in time, but he was going too fast, and the car began to skid. Turning the wheel into the skid, he righted the car and made it down the ramp. Minutes later he pulled into his driveway, waited for the garage door to open and coasted inside. Laying his head back again on the headrest, he remained in the car to settle his nerves. *I could've been killed out there.*

"Walter, is that you?" Mona called out from the kitchen door.

"Who else would it be?" he said slamming the car door. "You can be so irritating." He brushed by his wife and headed for the liquor cabinet.

"Dinner's almost ready. Was there any damage to our Florida house?"

"Mona, I just drove through a dangerous storm, passed cars in the ditch, the weatherman screaming at me to get off the road, and you ask me if I had time to take a leisurely stroll around the garden when I was in Port Orange."

"I thought—"

"That's the trouble with you, Mona. You don't think." He poured scotch, three-fingers high, into a glass.

"I thought you wanted champagne—"

"I'm not in the mood."

Mona floated over to the stove. A long organza coat revealed a deep V tank top in light-blue silk over matching Capris. Backless gold heels clung to her feet. She checked to see if the frozen stew had thawed. Stirring the mixture a few times, she put the lid back on the pot, went to the liquor cabinet beside the wet bar and fixed herself a double martini.

"What did that Detective Armstrong want?"

"He wanted to talk to me about Linda Darling's murder.

"What?"

They both looked around as the lights flickered but remained on. Mona slowly walked to the bank of picture windows overlooking their long expanse of lawn to the angry ocean, visibility limited by the beating rain. She stared at nothing.

"The detective said she was found in the canal across the street from our house," Falcon said between swallows of his drink.

"What did you say?" Mona turned her back to the raging storm and looked at her husband. "The canal? Does her brother know?"

"The detective didn't mention his name. I suggested to him that Joe Rocket could be involved with her death. From his reaction, I don't think he'd heard Joe's name before."

"Walter, I didn't know you had something to do with putting Joe in prison, other than testifying about his embezzlement of your funds."

"What? What are you saying?"

"Joe. You told me on the phone. You told me you framed him. Walter, do you think he would come after you? He knows about our house here in Maine."

"Very possible." Walter drained his drink and poured another. "When that officer guy came to the house to tell me that Linda was dead, I fixed a pot of coffee. When he left, I opened the dishwasher to put our coffee cups in and there was a mug, top rack. I'd bet your life that Joe had been in the house." *Mona's right. He could come after me. I've got to take care of Joe. No telling what he might do.* "We have to go back to Florida."

"Are you telling me summer is over?"

"I guess I am. I don't like Rocket nosing around and my not being there to take care of the business."

———

AFTER DINNER FALCON went to his den, shut the door, and pulled out his cell phone. Punching in the number, he gazed out the window waiting for the call to be picked up. He could not see the ocean the rain was so heavy.

Chapter 27

———

ELIZABETH SIGHED AS SHE helped herself to a small scoop of yellow rice and a piece of baked tilapia.

"Lizzy, is everything okay?" her dad said.

"You do seem a little preoccupied," Martha added, handing the bowl of salad greens to her husband.

"I met with Joe again."

"Joe?" Harry asked.

"Rocket. He apologized for lying to me. Said he didn't want me to be involved with a murder. His name is Joe Rocket just like Armstrong said, but it's a nickname of sorts. His real name is Joseph Sinclair Rockwell. Anyway, he asked me to do some investigating. Pass the tartar sauce, please."

"What did you say?" Harry set his knife and fork down on his plate, looked to his daughter for her answer.

"I thought about it for a few minutes, and then I said I would take the case...whatever that means."

"I hope he's going to pay you."

"Yes, he is, Mom. I'm okay with the arrangement so far. But, I have to warn you, that I can't discuss the particulars of the case with either of you. Client privilege you know."

"Oh, I see. Harry, more fish? Or a slice of pie?"

"If you'll excuse me, I'll eat the pie at my desk. There're some things I want to check out on the internet." Martha handed Elizabeth her dessert as she picked up her wine glass in the other hand.

"Alright, dear." Martha looked askance at her husband.

Elizabeth padded down the hall, white socks protecting her feet from the cold white tile floor. Entering her room, she bumped the door closed with a shake of her hip. Maggie made it into the room just in time pulling her tail in behind her.

Setting her plate and wine glass down on the desk, Elizabeth pushed the start button on her computer. Waiting for the desktop to display, she pulled out the pad with notes she had written after her meeting with the coroner.

"Okay, Miss PI, let's start earning your pay. I wonder if I'll be able to keep most of the $2000? Probably not unless I come up with something perfect."

Elizabeth pulled her wallet out of her tote. Carefully removing the two one-thousand-dollar bills, she smoothed them out on the glass that floated on top of her white wicker dresser. Snapping on the lamp by her bed, giving a creamy glow to the bedroom's pale yellow walls, she held one of the bills up to the light.

"Will you look at that, Maggie? It's the real thing. They stopped printing these a long time ago. I think I'll open a separate bank account tomorrow, you know, for business. Of course, if I don't get moving, I'll have to close it before I open it."

The computer ready, Elizabeth started her word processing program and typed a heading: "Case: Murder of Linda Darling."

Hitting the enter key, she typed another line: "Report Number One." Enter.

"Submitted by Elizabeth Stitchway, PI." Enter.

"Client: Joe Rocket."

She cocked her head as she looked at the beginning of her report. Pressing the enter key twice, she then typed the date. Taking a bite of her apple-pie, she set the fork down and began to type up her conversation with the coroner. She included his remarks about the blanket, perhaps Turkish. The wound indicating a .38 caliber gun caused it. She added the fact that Linda Darling's brother had identified the body and the comment from Sam Houston that he didn't think her brother was very upset—his sister lying dead on the slab with a bullet hole in her chest.

Elizabeth saved the document as: "Rocket Report 1."

Opening a new document she saved it as: "Assumptions and Actions." After a sip of wine, her fingers began to fly over the keyboard as thoughts filled her head. *Rocket thinks Falcon had a motive. Linda's brother not upset...could he have a motive? Could he be involved? Detective Armstrong says Joe Rocket is a person of interest. Maggie found Joe's shoe at the scene. Joe hates Falcon and is out for revenge. He says that Falcon framed him for embezzling funds. Linda, Joe, and Mr. Falcon were partners in the firm. That firm is no longer in business. Falcon started a new financial management company with Miss Darling.*

Elizabeth put her feet up on the bed. "And then there's that crazy, gun toting, ex-con Gus. You certainly didn't like him, Maggie." Elizabeth leaned forward to pet her dog. "You never stopped growling. But, did you notice Joe wasn't the least bit afraid or concerned, and the guy left when Joe asked him to. I bet he doesn't leave town...probably will hang around to help Joe stay 'outta trouble.' There certainly are a lot of players, Maggie. Where would Sherlock Holmes begin?" Elizabeth leaned back over to her desk, picking up the plate with one last bite of pie.

"I know. I'll stop in at the gun shop tomorrow. Take a look at a few guns that shoot a .38 caliber bullet. Ask them a few questions."

A piece of crust fell on her white T-shirt and another on her cut-off jean shorts. Brushing them away into the wastebasket.

"When dad was working he took me to the firing range." Maggie raised her head. "Yes, he did, and I got pretty good at hitting that man in the heart. If I'm going to be a real PI, I probably should buy a small pistol. All my online classes say that a PI must rely on stealth not guns. But, Maggie, we're talking murder here."

She leaned forward, patted Maggie on her silky head. Maggie inched forward a little accepting the caress, asking for more. "And, I think I'll go visit Miss Darling's brother...to offer my condolences, being as I found her."

Elizabeth heard a tap on her door. "Come on in," she called out.

Her dad rolled in. "I brought you a cup of tea. Your mother is a little upset you didn't eat dessert with us."

"I'm sorry, Dad. My head was spinning. I had to type up my thoughts."

"If you ever want to talk, have someone to bounce ideas off of, you know where to find me." He smiled at his daughter, performed a perfect wheelie and left her room.

Elizabeth attacked her keyboard again, typing out her to-do list. Under each heading, she added several questions. Elizabeth read her report once more to be sure she hadn't left anything out. Satisfied, she closed the file and turned off her computer.

She scratched around the bottom of her backpack.

"Where's that napkin with Joe's number? Come on. Come on, where is it?" She dumped the contents of the backpack on her bed, spreading the contents over the pale-yellow quilt with white cabbage roses.

"Would you look at all this stuff, Maggie. Here's a biscuit for you." Maggie gratefully caught the morsel in the air and again sat down, waiting for another treat. "Here it is, Maggie. What kind of an investigator would I be if I lost my client's number? I'd better store it right now on my phone. Backup. Backup. Always have a backup plan."

"Hello, Mr. Rocket?"

"Stitch?"

"Stitch. That's the second time you've called me that. I rather like it, you know, for my business card...A stitch in time saves nine. Nice ring to it don't you think?"

"Only too glad to help."

"Yes. I guess we sound a little different on the phone. Mr. Rocket, I have my first report for you. And, just so you know, I'm keeping a meticulous record of my time."

"Miss Stitchway," Joe said mimicking Elizabeth's no-nonsense tone, "of course, I expect a breakdown of your time billed against the retainer, say at the end of the month. Naturally, we both have to agree that you must also come up with some information."

"Naturally. Well then, I will proceed with my report...are you aware that the end of the month is in a week? Six days to be precise."

"Fine. I don't have a calendar in front of me, but if you say it's in six days, then the end of the month is in six days. Now tell me what you have."

"Report Number One, submitted by Elizabeth Stitchway, PI. Client: Joe Rocket—"

"Don't read your report, just summarize what it contains."

"Well, alright, but I don't want to skip anything."

"Stitch, it's not in your DNA to skip *anything*!"

Chuckling, she replied, "I guess you're right, Joe. Well, I went back to the morgue."

"The morgue?"

"Yes, to talk to the coroner. He's a very nice gentleman, Australian. Anyway, I said I was in the neighborhood and wondered if anybody had claimed the body. Following is my first piece of information for you, Mr. Rocket. He said that her brother had come to the morgue. In fact, he was worried about his sister and had finally called the police to file a missing-person report. Detective Armstrong referred him to the morgue to see if he could identify Jane Doe. Mr. Darling went to the morgue and identified Jane Doe as his sister Miss Linda Darling."

"We already knew who she was. Detective—"

"But, we didn't know that it was her brother who had ID'd her."

"Very good, Stitchway."

"There's more, lots. When I said to Dr. Houston, that's the coroner, that her brother must have been upset, he said 'not really.' His exact words—'not really.' Joe, maybe he killed his sister?"

"Unlikely, but interesting. Go on."

"Well, I asked about the blanket she was wrapped in. Sam thought it was Turkish from the weave and the pattern, quite expensive."

"I know the blanket."

"You do?"

"Yes, there's one just like it over the back of the couch in Falcon's living room. I bought the blankets on a trip to Turkey when I visited the country to check out the rules for trading stocks in their market."

"Mr. Rocket, that piece of information is not good for you."

"Miss Stitchway, that was eight years ago. The house has been in Falcon's possession since I was imprisoned, and when I returned to Port Orange on the freight train, the first thing I did was to help you out of the canal."

"Oh. Well, okay. Maybe."

"I also knew the victim in the blanket was Linda when I pulled her out of the water. With the arm dangling out of the blanket, I recognized the ring on her finger."

"You never gave any indication that—"

"I know. I was shocked. There was no way I could stick around and explain how I knew her. What else?"

"Well, let's see after that curve ball you just threw at me...I mentioned the nasty hole in Miss Darling's chest. Sam said it looked like maybe a .38 caliber bullet could have done it. When I asked if he found the bullet, he said no, that he had not performed an autopsy yet, but there was an exit wound in her back. It went clear through the body. Mr. Rocket, are you still there?"

"Yes. Go on."

"The only thing I found out was that the name of Miss Darling's brother is—"

"Timothy."

"Why, yes. Do you know him?"

"Yah, I met him a few times. I pegged him as a leech. Right after Linda and Walter and I started our hedge fund company, he moved in with Linda. Didn't even ask her. She went home one day, and there he was...car in the garage, clothes in the closet, shaving gear in the bathroom."

"That takes chutzpa."

"Yah...hang on a minute."

Elizabeth scanned her to do list while she waited for Joe to come back on the line.

"Stitch?"

"I'm here."

"Gus just popped in. He's getting to be a regular Mary Poppins. He wanted to know if the dolly that would be you noticed a black car following you?"

"Joe, do you know how many black cars there are in Port Orange?"

"I know. I know, but Gus is pretty good at spotting these things. Anyway, keep your eyes open and, Stitch—"

"Yes?"

"Good work."

Chapter 28

———

THE OFFICER APPROACHED the blonde receptionist. She finished transferring a call from the console at her desk and looked up at her visitor. "May I help you, sir?"

"Yes. My name is Detective Armstrong, Port Orange Police Department. I'm looking for Mr. Falcon. Is he in?" Armstrong flashed his badge.

"Oh, I'm sorry. Mr. Falcon is away for the summer. Can someone else help you?"

"I'm looking for some information on Linda Darling. I believe she worked with Mr. Falcon?"

"Oh, yes, sir. Tragic. Very tragic. Mr. Falcon asked me to forward any questions concerning Miss Darling to our financial analyst Mr. Scott. He's just finishing up an appointment. Would you like to speak with him?"

"Yes, I would. I'll wait." Armstrong sauntered over to a sitting area on his right, thick green carpet cushioning his footsteps. He eased himself into an over-stuffed armchair, part of a grouping with a couch around a smoky-glass coffee table. Trees softened the lobby space ringed with windows and a vaulted ceiling reaching to the heavens. A free-standing fountain provided a pleasing sound as water gently flowed over a rock formation. *I guess this is all supposed to calm the frazzled nerves of investors trying to keep from going broke,* Armstrong thought. Looking down, he wiped a speck of dust off his right shoe.

"Hello, Detective Armstrong, I believe?" The young man strolled up to the officer, extended his hand, and firmly shook Armstrong's. "My name is Charles Scott. I understand you're inquiring about Miss Darling?"

Armstrong nodded, taking note of the age of the man. *Young to be in this business. I don't think I'd take his advice...if I were looking for it.*

"Come with me, Detective. We can talk privately in my office." Armstrong followed the boy down a warm-gray hall lined with paintings of sailboats, their sails straining from the force of the wind, others tethered to an anchor off some shore.

Entering the spacious office, the man gestured Armstrong to take a seat in front of his ornate, carved-cherry desk. *Business must be good.* "Mr. Scott, what exactly is your position in this firm?"

"What? I thought you wanted to talk about Miss Darling. For your information, I'm a senior investment advisor. But what possible relevance is my position in the company?"

"I just want to establish your relationship, how you fit into the picture with Mr. Falcon and Miss Darling."

"Look, Mr. Falcon asked me to answer any questions about Linda...like how long she worked here, where she lived, did she have any enemies, any friends. Nothing more."

"Alright. Did she have any enemies?"

"Lots."

"Could you give me some names?"

"Everybody. Nobody liked her. She was very bossy. You can get a list of employees from our personnel manager and everyone on it disliked her."

"I see. I guess that pretty much rules out any friends. How did you get along with her, Mr. Scott?"

"Well, she was very bossy as I said. Never gave me the time of day. Under all that highfalutin glamorous exterior beat a heart of stone."

"If nobody cared for Miss Darling, why do you suppose she stayed at the firm?"

"The clients loved her. She brought in *a lot* of money."

"I thought you said nobody liked her."

"I was a bit harsh. She and I locked horns—it never mattered what I did, it was wrong in her eyes. Too bad though—she was a looker."

"I see, then not everybody disliked her?"

"I guess you could say that. She acted differently with her clients. Pretending to be buddy-buddy like. Maybe that's why they liked her. Here's her address. My secretary printed out this sheet for anybody asking for information. Her phone number is there as well. I'm sure her brother will answer. He moved in with her some time ago, but I've never met him. You'll have to excuse me now, Detective. My next scheduled appointment is here, and I don't want to keep her waiting. She's one of Walter's, Mr. Falcon's, best clients. Besides, as you can see, I don't have any information other than what's on that piece of paper."

Chapter 29

———

ELIZABETH WAS NOW LOCKED into the case—finding Linda Darling's killer and thereby freeing Joe from suspicion unless she found out that he murdered her. But she was proceeding on the premise that he was innocent. Pulling her slight frame up to its full five-foot three-and-three-quarters inches, she pushed open the door, entering the Florida Gun Exchange. She was surprised at the number of salespeople—at least six, five men and one woman. *Just look at all the customers lined up in front of the cases. And moreover at those rifles. Business be must good.*

She looked around, casually strolled to the case by the female clerk packing a gun on her hip. She was on the phone, asking questions. Finishing her conversation, the clerk wrote a few notes on a pad of paper and then turned to face Elizabeth.

"Hello. May I help you?" she asked. Her smile was open and friendly, but she was muscular, and Elizabeth couldn't help thinking that she would not want to pick a fight with this person.

"Yes, I'm interested in buying a gun for protection. I thought maybe something in a thirty-eight caliber." She looked straight into the clerk's eyes daring her to make fun of her. The woman gave no indication of being surprised at Elizabeth's request, and in fact seemed eager to help her.

"I have several you can take a look at. Have you ever fired a gun?"

"About five years ago with my dad, he was head of security at a company until he hurt his back. Anyway, he took me to a range a few times. I got to be pretty good at hitting the target. He said I was a natural."

"It sounds like it. Let's take a look at a Smith & Wesson. They have a line of handguns designed for women—the guns have small frames, compact. The Lady Smith should fit your hand nicely." She motioned to Elizabeth to follow her.

"Here, see how this feels to you," the woman said pulling a handgun from the case, laying it in Elizabeth's hand. "It's a .38 special, holds five rounds."

"It's nice and light." Elizabeth looked it over, lifting it a couple of times in the air, running her finger over the wood-grained grip, touching the cold metal barrel. "I guess this could put a bullet right through a person."

"You got that right."

"I know there's a three-day waiting period, but what about a concealed-weapon permit?"

"We have a two-hour firearms class followed by a morning at the firing range. Then you can apply for the permit."

"Sounds good. And concealed means I—"

"Can carry the weapon on your person, in the car, or at home."

"You've been very helpful..."

"My name's Donna."

"And I'm Elizabeth. Let's get started on the paperwork. I'm going to follow your advice...this Lady Smith is perfect."

Elizabeth left the gun shop and headed for the address she found in the telephone book. The address for L. Darling. It was the only Darling in the book, so she was sure it had to be Linda's.

"Now, do I call to see if her brother's there or do I just go knock on the door?" Puzzling which way to handle the situation, fifteen minutes later she arrived at Linda Darling's address. She drove to the end of the street, made a U-turn, and pulled over to the curb across from the house—nice, upscale, coral-stucco over cement block. It was trimmed in cream including two pillars on either side of the covered entrance, all giving the entry an elegant look. "Sherlock, what would you do? Probably not barge up to the door."

Rooting around her lime-green-and pink-candy-stripe canvas bag, she pulled out her cell phone, punched the numbers she had copied from the phone book.

"Hello," the male voice said.

Dropping the phone on the floor of the car, Elizabeth quickly bent over to retrieve it. "Hello. Is this the Darling residence?"

"Yes, it is. Who's this?"

"My name is Elizabeth Stitchway. I'm looking for Linda Darling's brother, Timothy. Are you by any chance Timothy?"

"Yes, what do you want?"

"Mr. Darling I was just in the neighborhood, and I thought I might stop by to offer my condolences. I'm the lady who pulled your sister's body out of the canal."

"Oh, my. Yes. Where are you? Please do stop by."

"Actually, I'm parked across the street. I didn't know if you would be...I'll come right over." *Sherlock, what do you think? Not bad, huh?*

"Come in, Miss Stitchway. I thought we might talk in the kitchen. I was just having some tea. Would you care for a cup?"

"That would be nice." Elizabeth stepped into the foyer, her eyes drawn through the great room to a bank of windows, and out to a pond. She followed Timothy toward the picture windows, but he turned right to an open kitchen with an island topped with pink-granite.

Elizabeth put her bag on an empty bar chair at the island. "I'm truly sorry about your sister. Were you close?" she asked perching on the high chair beside her bag.

"Oh, yes. She was very kind to me. When I lost my job as a salesman at a trucking firm, she took me right in, insisted actually."

"That was kind. Have Mr. Rocket or Mr. Falcon called you? I read in the paper that she currently worked with Mr. Falcon, and earlier with a Mr. Rocket. Strange name."

"I believe Rocket is in prison. Some kind of embezzlement from the company he and my sister and Mr. Falcon formed. I know she was furious at the time. She lost a lot of money as did her group of clients. Too bad, because I always thought she had an interest in Joe. I don't believe I saw the article you referred to, Miss Stitchway."

"Please, call me Elizabeth. You were saying your sister was interested in Mr. Rocket?" Elizabeth took a sip of her tea and leaned forward resting on her elbows.

"Romantic. In fact, I think she really fell hard for him, but I guess he wasn't interested. I remember her saying that all he cared about was money, lots of money. I always told her that wasn't a bad thing...wanting money. Mr. Falcon, on the other hand, was a totally different story."

"How's that? Nice tea by the way. Mind if I pour some more? May I refresh your cup?"

"Yes, please. Oh, I forgot the lemon. I always like lemon with my tea don't you?"

"Always."

Timothy went to the refrigerator and opened a small plastic container of lemon wedges. "Here you are, Miss...Elizabeth. I must say I'm glad you stopped by. It's very lonely here...without my sister."

"I'm sure it must be. You were saying about Mr. Falcon."

"Oh, Yes. At first, Walt was very nice, charming even, almost to the point of buttering me up like I could help him win over my sister. Ha! That was a laugh. She chased both Falcon and Rocket relentlessly. Like I said, I think she really loved Joe, but she wanted Falcon's money."

"But isn't Mr. Falcon married?"

"Yeah, but that didn't seem to slow him down. If his wife was up in Maine, he'd come back to Port Orange for some reason, and Linda would spend every night with him. I think he was just after her body, if you know what I mean."

"Oh, yes, I know what you mean, Mr. Darling."

"Please, call me Timothy. Did you ever learn who helped you get my sister out of the canal?"

"What makes you think somebody helped me?"

"The medical examiner. When the detective asked me to go to the morgue to see if I could identify the body, he explained how you and a man found her."

"Oh, I see. In fact, I did bump into the man...at the dog park. A Mr. Price. That was his name. You have a lovely view, Timothy. I see there's a picture of Mr. Falcon. Is that your sister with him?"

"Yes, and Joe...much happier days."

"Are you planning a funeral for your sister?"

"No point right now. Not until they release her body. I wish they'd hurry up. Actually I contracted with a funeral home to cremate her as soon as possible. Those were her wishes. There'll be no memorial either. Our parents are deceased, and Falcon hasn't shown any interest. Her clients...well, nothing I can do about them."

"What are you going to do with this beautiful house?"

"Live in it. Linda hoped Walt would buy it for her, so she put the minimum down. She told me she was sure Walt was going to get a divorce and marry her someday. Then she'd sell this place."

"Oh, that would have been terrible for you. What would you have done?"

"That's just it...I would have been out on the street."

"But, Timothy, are you working?"

"No, but I do have an interview set up with Volusia County Trucking next week. Of course, once Linda's insurance pays off, as her only heir, I won't ever have to work again. More tea, Miss Stitchway?"

———

ELIZABETH LEFT TIMOTHY. *Fascinating fellow,* she thought. *A leech I believe is how Joe characterized him.*

Finding the telephone number she wanted, Elizabeth placed the call.

"Volusia County Trucking. May I help you?"

"Oh, yes, please. I'm calling for my friend, Timothy Darling. He just suffered a sprained ankle, and he wanted me to let you know he may have to reschedule his interview with you next week."

"I'm sorry, but we aren't hiring right now. Perhaps you have the wrong trucking company."

"I'll check again. Thank you anyway." Elizabeth tossed her cell into her tote and headed to meet her parents for dinner. *So, Timothy, why did you lie to me?*

———

A BLACK SEDAN WAS parked next to the curb at the end of the block. The driver appeared to be sleeping, but when the yellow coupe took off down the street, the sedan moved along as well, but not too close.

Chapter 30

—

ELIZABETH BREEZED INTO the restaurant feeling like a million bucks in her coral Capris topped with a spray of matching daylilies on a white T. Looking around for her parents, she spotted them out on the deck overlooking the Halifax River enjoying the evening breeze off the water. This dinner was a celebration of sorts. Her dad had been given the go-ahead by his physical therapist to walk a little each day—but no stairs. Elizabeth quickly joined them at their table, blowing each a kiss as she sat down. A glass of Chardonnay sat in front of her.

"Thanks, Dad. Umm, nice and cold. I bought you a present."

"A present…it's not my birthday."

"Very funny, Dad. Think of it as a reward for working so hard on your exercises and now you're walking. Here, try this cane on for size. It's a replica of Dr. House's, you know, the TV series. He calls it his flaming cane…it was designed for him."

"Lizzy, this is great." Harry stood up, took a few steps. Smiling at Martha, raising his eyebrows, he nodded down at the cane. "With the flames around the lower half, I'll be hot to trot. No stopping me now." Harry sat down hooking the cane over the back of his chair. He tapped his daughter's wine glass with his. "Thanks, Lizzy."

"You're certainly chipper," Martha said to her daughter. "You must have had a good day."

"I did…a busy one. After work, I visited a gun shop, the one up on Ridgewood Avenue and put an order in for a little pistol, and I—"

"You what?" Martha said, looking around to be sure the people sitting at the table next to them hadn't heard her raise her voice.

Elizabeth leaned forward and whispered, "Mom, I'm working a case, a murder case. When I'm on the job, I feel I need protection."

"Well, this is the first I've heard about your working on a real case, and informing us not just any case, but a murder. That hurricane brought nothing but trouble," Martha whispered. "I hope to goodness you didn't quit your job at the post office. You'd better not take a gun in there, or you'll be the one who lands in jail. Harry, did you know about this, this case?" Martha looked sharply at her husband.

Harry sat up straight with an amused twinkle in his eyes as he watched the byplay. "Not exactly, but we both knew she was cooking up something. What model did you pick out, Lizzy?"

"Harry, don't encourage the girl."

"Dad, it's really cute, it—"

"Cute? Really, Elizabeth, this is just too much. I don't want that gun in the house."

"Mom, I'm not a little girl. In case you haven't noticed, I've grown up. I'm thirty-one, and if I want a pistol when I'm on a job, I'll have a pistol. If you don't want a gun in the house, and I feel I need one, then maybe it's time I find my own apartment. Now that dad's on his feet you won't need my help so much anyway."

"Elizabeth, please lower your voice, people are looking at us." Martha raised the menu pretending to look at the list of entrées.

"Now listen, you two, let's put this conversation on hold until we get home. The waiter is coming our way, and I for one plan to enjoy my dinner."

————

"LIZZY, CAN I COME IN?" Harry asked pushing the door open a crack.

"Of course, Dad. Here, sit on my chair. I've finished my report. It's so good to see you walking again."

"I'm not going to win any races yet, but I swear my legs are getting stronger with each step. The therapist says not to overdo, but it was beyond wonderful when I walked into the restaurant with your mother today, albeit a little slow."

"You did good, Dad. You looked strong, not hunched over when we left the restaurant."

"I felt good, and that cane gives me confidence, helps me feel steady. Lizzy, I didn't realize you were so involved in this case. Did you take that Mr. Rocket up on his offer—finding the killer of that body you two found in the canal? You haven't said much since we last talked?"

"Yes. I have two, maybe three suspects. Joe Rocket hired me as his PI. I asked him for a retainer like it was expected. He laid out the money immediately. Took it right out of his wallet—two one-thousand-dollar bills. (same as earlier. Out of circulation since 1969. Left it) Can you imagine walking around with cash like that? Mom never took me seriously, but you did. You know I've wanted to go out on my own, to be a private investigator. But I didn't think I could do it, and then people said it wasn't a job for a woman, and well, all that stuff I told you about with my being made fun of in school, I just let my idea dangle out there...a dream. But then I started to build my confidence when I worked some assignments for Mr. Goodwurthy."

"Lizzy, I'm sure you have to have a license to be a professional PI in Florida."

"I know, Dad. I checked. I have to have two years of full-time experience before I can even qualify for a license. Verifiable experience."

"What about your assignments with Goodwurthy? Will they count?"

"No, because so far it's been part-time. Some of my university classes will help, however. No matter how you look at it, two years on the job would be best. Besides, working for an investigative company will be extremely valuable—like an internship."

"Then you can get a license?" Harry asked.

"Not quite, there's an examination I have to pass. I'm told it covers the parts of Florida law that deal directly with the business practices of being a PI and my legal responsibilities."

"Two years will fly by, Lizzy. Especially if you're doing something you like, and, if you find it's not for you...well, you'll never know unless you try. Working as a PI could be dangerous, which I'm sure you realize, or you wouldn't be purchasing a gun. But remember, a gun can also be trouble."

"You were a big influence on me, Dad. Remember, you'd take me to your company some evenings and always on Sunday when you made your rounds. The guards on duty showed you great respect...and they were all packing. Some of the guns looked huge, at least to me."

"Yes, we were armed. It was a form of intimidation to any bad guys to stay away. You were so young...I never realized how impressionable you were."

"But, Dad, the best was when you took me to the practice range. I'll never forget the day you handed me your gun and told me to shoot at the target."

Harry chuckled. "The first time you pulled the trigger, the kick almost knocked you on your keister—"

"Hey, even though you warned me, the force of the kickback caught me off guard."

"You were taking classes at the university...what, you were twenty-three?"

"Yup, twenty-three and on my way to becoming a police officer until—"

"Never you mind about Arthur and all that other bullying stuff. I think you're back on track. You still have a lot to learn, Lizzy, and I think you should continue your studies, part-time anyway."

"Oh, I will. I'm already putting together a five-year plan."

"Five-year plan? I remember when I laid out my plan...that was some time ago. When do you pick up your pistol? And, you never did say what you picked out."

"Three days. The waiting period. I met this ex-cop at the gun shop. She was very helpful and suggested the Lady Smith—"

"Ah, a Smith and Wesson."

"She said the company designed it for women."

"Maybe we can go to the range together...just like old times."

"I'd like that. Dad, what I said at the restaurant, about moving out...it's not that I don't appreciate what you and mom have done for me, letting me live here. Plus I felt I could help after you were hurt so badly."

"Lizzy, it's I who owe you thanks for staying with us and don't worry about your mother. She'll come around. She just doesn't want you to get hurt."

"Tomorrow, after I return my truck to the yard, I'm going to start looking for a place to live...on my own."

———

THE LIGHTS WENT OUT for the night in the Stitchway house and the black sedan, no lights, slowly cruised by dissolving into the night air.

Chapter 31

———

"SMITTY, WHAT THE HELL are you thinking...coming to my house?" Falcon rubbed his forehead, pacing back and forth in his office.

"Hey, pal, if you'll stop charging around the room, I'll tell you why. Is the missus home?"

"No. She's out grocery shopping. We drove in last night, and the first thing she was quick to inform me of was that we were out of coffee. Now hurry up and say what you've got to say and then get out. I gave you an assignment which did not include coming to my house."

"This is a very risky deal. I don't know where Rocket is. He has to be hiding out somewhere. I've been tailing that mail lady but so far nothing. Tell me, Walt, what's he got on you that you want him eliminated? Tell me that and then maybe I can figure out where he is."

"The why is none of your business. I hired you for a job. If you can't find it in that black heart of yours to pull it off, let me know, and I'll find somebody who can."

"I'll do it, don't get yourself so worked up. However, I want half now and the balance when the job is done, or I say goodbye."

"Geez, you've got to be kidding. You know I'm good for it."

"Eight grand now, Walter, or there's no deal."

"Okay, okay, but then I don't want to see your ugly puss again until you've kept your side of the bargain, and never again in my house." Falcon went to the painting behind his desk, tripped the latch, and swung the frame away from the wall. Twirling the combination, at the final click he pulled open the safe's small steel door.

"What the hell is this?" Lying on the bottom of the safe was an envelope with his name on it. Pulling the paper out, he unfolded the letter. His hand began to tremble. The message was short and to the point.

> Falcon,
> I cleaned out your stash. Consider this money a down payment on the thousands you owe me. Your days are numbered.
> Rocket

"That bastard." Falcon slammed the safe door shut, swung the painting back in place, and sat down in his favorite chair. Pulling a handkerchief from his shorts pocket, he mopped the beads of perspiration forming on his brow.

"What's the matter, Walter?"

"It seems I've had a visitor. I can't give you the money right now. Come by my office in the morning. Don't give your name to the receptionist. Just say I'm expecting you. Now get out of here."

"Not so fast. Do you have any idea where I can find this guy? He seems to have gone underground."

"How should I know? That's part of what you're being paid for—to find the bastard. Shit, you've been tailing the mail lady, why don't you stop her, ask if she knows where the man is who helped her drag the body out of the canal that night. Geez, do I have to think of everything?"

"Something's up with that broad. She paid a visit to Linda Darling's brother. Why would she do that?"

"Probably so she could offer him sympathy, stupid."

"Well, I'm playing the angle that between the two of them, Rocket will surface."

"I told the police I think Joe killed Linda." Falcon leaned his head back and closed his eyes.

"Yah, he could've. From what you told me, he had a motive, but he has a bigger one to take you out. You act like he has a real vendetta."

"I'm glad you're enjoying my predicament."

Hearing the garage door open, Falcon sprang to his feet. "Now get out of here and do your job, so I can get on with my life."

"Okay, okay, I'm going."

Mona came down the hall as Falcon let the curtain fall back into place, making sure his visitor was out of sight.

"Who was that, Walt? It looked like Smitty. I saw his bald head from the back as the garage door was closing."

"It was Smitty."

"What's the matter with you? You don't look right. Did he give you some bad news?"

"No. Nothing's the matter. I'm going to lay down a minute. But first I have to get something."

Walter strolled to the garage, shut the door behind him and turned on the overhead light. Listening to be sure Mona didn't follow him, he hesitated then pulled down the attic stairs. Climbing up to the open space, he stopped before stepping onto the plywood flooring. The garage light wasn't strong enough to see over to the rafter where he had hidden the box.

Falcon climbed back down, retrieved a flashlight from the workbench and climbed back up, this time walking straight to the hiding place. Relieved the box was still where he put it, he left the attic and returned to the bedroom.

Falcon rubbed his chest, worried he felt the onslaught of chest pains. *I'll just take a little rest,* he thought. *Figure out how to protect myself from Rocket.* He laid down on the bed and closed his eyes. "Ah, that's better." His eyes flew open. "What the—"

"I brought you a glass of champagne, Walter. We didn't get a chance to celebrate in Maine. Remember, you said to put some champagne on ice for a celebration."

"Mona, you've been drinking. I don't want any champagne."

"Walter, let's start over. Let's leave Florida. We have enough money. Linda's gone. Who cares about Rocket!"

Mona removed her chiffon duster, revealing a blue satin nightgown clinging to her body, a deep V showing her ample breasts pressing against the silky fabric. Falcon jumped off the bed knocking the champagne glass out of Mona's hand. He stomped to the door, turned to look at his wife. Tears were streaming down her cheeks, dropping onto the blue satin, streaking the gown.

"I don't love you, Mona. I never loved you. Pull yourself together. I'm going to have my lawyer draw up divorce papers."

Chapter 32

———

ARMSTRONG WAS STANDING just shy of the surf. A kid, bare feet, dark blue t-shirt with Surfer's Delight screened over a surfboard, ran toward him. The boy's blonde hair, tied in a tight ponytail, swinging as he ran.

"Hi, Detective," he said, laying his board on the sand and taking a quick look around for his friends.

"Hello, young fella. Nice board. You called asking me to meet you. You have some information for me?"

"Yah, as I said on the phone, I heard you talking to that shithead Scott about Linda Darling. I was cleaning the baseboards just outside of the office. I do that from time to time—"

"Eavesdrop?"

"I like to think of it more as job security. Anyway, he didn't give you the real skinny about Falcon and his babe Linda."

"His babe?"

"Oh, yah...right there in the office—many times—if you know what I mean."

"Uh, Larry's your name?"

"Larry Richards. I've worked at Mr. Falcon's company as a cleaner off and on after school for the past three years."

"Other than their *doing it* in the office, what else did you see?"

"Hey, Detective, I'm not a peeper. I didn't *see* them, I *heard* them. I heard plenty. Linda Darling, perfect name, by the way, threatened Mr. Falcon if he didn't divorce his wife and marry her."

"Threatened him with what?"

"That I don't know. All I know is that he yelled at her, calling her a whore. She was definitely pissed, and she gave it right back at him. Said he'd be sorry if he didn't dump his wife."

A group of kids rushed to the water with their boards. "Come on, Larry. The waves are perfect."

"Gotta go, Detective." Larry stripped off his shirt and rumpled cut-off jeans, leaving them on the sand as he ran into the surf with his board.

Armstrong called after him. "If you hear or see anything more you think I should know, call me. I guess you have my number."

Armstrong watched the group of young people paddle out on the surf, heading for the breaking waves. "Must be nice to play without a care in the world." He hiked up his trousers and strode on the packed sand to his unmarked car. Parking on the beach, unless there was a storm, was a privilege the area residents and tourists took advantage of whenever they had the opportunity.

He smiled looking over the crowded beach. He was the only one in black, and the only one in long pants. Many on the force wore shorts in the summer, but he preferred his signature uniform: black shirt, black trousers, and black gun belt. Everyone, however, wore dark glasses to protect their eyes from the blazing sun.

Sitting in his unmarked car, Armstrong pulled his hand over his balding head. Frustrated, he shook a cigarette out of the pack he kept in his breast pocket. He never lit up but liked the comfort of knowing he could if he wanted to. He put the filter tip between his lips...exhaled a sigh looking out at the sparkling ocean. *I'm getting nowhere. Linda Darling's circle of friends or enemies, depending on who's talking, is small. And everybody says they know nothing. Well, someone's lying.*

Twenty minutes later, he found himself in front of Falcon's house. Pulling his cell phone out of his pants pocket, he punched in the number. A woman answered on the fourth ring.

"Hello, this is Detective Armstrong. Is Mr. Falcon home?"

"No, he's at work."

"I see. Are you Mrs. Falcon?"

"Yes."

"I'm outside, across the street. Might I have a word with you?"

"Oh, I don't know…my husband—"

"I won't keep you long. Just a few questions."

"Alright."

Armstrong jammed the damp cigarette into his shirt pocket and started up the walkway. Mona met him at the door and motioned for him to come in.

"Please call me Mona, Detective. We can sit here in the living room."

Although it was early afternoon, Armstrong thought Mrs. Falcon looked like she just got out of bed. Her hair wasn't combed, her face drawn, circles under her eyes. Even so, he could see she was a beautiful woman.

"Care for a drink, Detective?"

"No thanks. I'm on the citizen's dime, but thanks for the offer. Don't let me stop you though."

"I had just made a fresh martini when you called." Mona went to the table behind the sofa and picked up her cocktail. "Now, what can I do for you, Detective Armstrong?"

"Did you know Linda Darling? I'm sure your husband has told you about her body being found in the canal across the street from your house."

"Yes, he did mention the matter, and yes, I knew Miss Darling. But that's it—I rarely saw her. She was my husband's business partner."

"What about Joe Rocket?"

"What about him?"

"Were you friends?"

Mona laughed. "Excuse me for laughing. Joe Rocket didn't have any women friends, only business associates."

"Have you seen him recently?"

"I understand he was just released from prison, but no, I haven't seen him."

"Well, I guess that does it. You have a lovely home, Mrs. Falcon. Nice touch that blanket over the back of the couch. The colors are striking."

"Yes, it's one of the leftovers from Rocket's things. My husband bought this house from Joe before he went to prison. As I understand the story, Joe bought the blanket on one of his trips to Turkey."

——

DETECTIVE ARMSTRONG DROVE out of Turtle Grove Estates. Shaking his head, he mumbled, "You talk to someone, ask a few questions, and what do you get, more questions. Well, that's two interesting conversations today, why not make it three."

Pulling into the CVS drugstore parking lot, he turned to his onboard computer and found the address he was looking for. Ten minutes later he stood on the Darling's doorstep ringing the bell.

A disheveled Timothy Darling opened the door. "Detective, let's see it's been a little over a week since we met at the morgue. Foul place." Timothy leaned on the door, bare feet sticking out from under his jeans. His breath smelled of liquor. Even though it was almost cocktail time, he obviously had a good head start. "What can I do for you? Or, are you going to do something for me, like getting my sister's body released."

Armstrong stood his ground in spite of the bad odor. "I was in the neighborhood, so I thought I'd see how you were doing and I'd like to ask you a few questions."

"A social call, how nice. Come on in. Just let me turn off the TV."

Timothy swayed a little as he walked to the television, snapped it off with the remote, but not before Armstrong saw that Timothy Darling had been watching a pornographic movie.

"Would you like to join me for a drink, Detective? I'm going to get a refill."

"No thanks. On the job you know."

Armstrong followed Timothy into the kitchen and took a seat at the island.

"Seems everyone wants to say how sorry they are. Not many days ago that nice mail lady sat right where you're sitting now and said the same thing."

So, I seem to be a few steps behind Elizabeth, Armstrong thought. Sam's right. That new PI is certainly digging for information. I wonder where else she's been?

"But, Detective, only a handful of people have called from my sister's company. And, then it was all business. I shouldn't be surprised, though. Nobody liked her."

"When did you last see your sister?"

"The day she died, or rather the day she went missing, but I didn't know she was missing at the time, not until I called you and you invited me to meet you at the morgue. Nasty place. Sure you won't join me, Detective. No fun drinking alone."

Chapter 33

———

"BYE, HELEN. Have a good run. Watch out for the gators." Elizabeth laughed as she passed her friend on the way out to the yard to pack her truck.

"Back at you, Lizzy."

Twenty minutes later Elizabeth was stuffing mailboxes. She looked down at her purple flowered bag. *The News Journal* stuck out of one end. "Plan for the day. During lunch break, circle all possible apartments and, if time, call the contact listed in the ad." Now that she was working on a case, she found herself talking as if typing up a report.

Approaching the canal, she noticed a black Ford Taurus parked beside the road. A short, rotund man with a fringe of gray hair circling a bald spot waved her down. She stopped alongside where he stood.

"Need some help, mister?"

"Hello, miss. I'm a reporter for the Orlando Sentinel, and I've been sent to ask you some questions about the night of the hurricane."

"Okay, but I can only give you a minute. I haven't finished my deliveries."

"Are you the mail lady who was blown into the ditch the day of the big storm?"

"Yes. But that certainly isn't news."

"It's been reported that you said there was a man who helped you. I was wondering if you've seen him recently."

"Look, mister, if you have questions about the case, I suggest you talk to the police. What's your name anyway and I'd like to see your press badge."

"Sorry, lady, I just wanta talk to the guy. If you haven't seen him, I guess I'll just have to try someone else. Catch you later."

"Reporter my eye. How'd you like that, Sherlock. 'Let me see your press badge' I said." Elizabeth turned onto Red Snapper Lane. The Falcon's garage door was open, and Mrs. Falcon was lifting grocery bags out of the trunk of her car. Elizabeth pulled next to mailbox 8236, grabbed an extra pack of circulars, and headed at a trot to talk to the woman.

"Hello, Mrs. Falcon. You're back early. Do you want me to start delivering your mail tomorrow?"

"Oh, hi. Yes, yes, that would be okay. Go ahead...bring the mail."

"Hold on a sec. Let me get a new card from my truck. I'll need your signature to cancel the instructions to forward your mail to Maine and to resume your deliveries here."

Elizabeth ran to the truck, picked up a blank card and ran back to Mrs. Falcon. "Here you go. Let

me check the boxes for you. There. Just sign by the X."

Mona did as she was told and handed the signed card and pen back to Elizabeth.

"You cut your time up north short this year. Too many tourists?"

"No. We just wanted to get back. The past few weeks have been rather stressful. We found we were going back and forth so much. The third time, we said enough. Let's stay home."

"At least you missed the hurricane."

"Yes, we were here just three days when we heard the warnings that a possible hurricane was coming. Walter was attending a two-day business meeting in Tampa. He called me to pack up. He said clouds were beginning to build in the Gulf and he thought we'd better leave before we were trapped here. Thanks for the circulars."

Elizabeth finished her deliveries and headed back to the post office to drop off the truck and pick up her car. Her workday over, she drove to a group of fast-food restaurants and parked in a space by Panera Bread. The temperature had eased off a bit, and the thought of an icy soda at one of their outdoor tables shaded from the sun would be perfect while she scanned the ads for available apartments.

There were two ads for a one-bedroom rental that caught her eye. She connected with an answering machine in both cases and left her name and cell number, and that she was interested in the apartment advertised in the newspaper. Sipping her soda, her mind wandered, decorating her new place. *The closet will have to be big enough for shelves, lots of shelves. A shelf for all my totes, another for the Ts, and one more for my Capris. I'll fold everything, so the edge of each piece is facing me. It'll be so easy to color coordinate. With only a few dresses I don't need much room for hangers.*

Sitting back in the black-metal chair, she glanced at the bushes enclosing the patio and then on out to the parking lot. She saw a man, short and balding, looking her way. "Why, there's that fake reporter!"

Grabbing her cell phone, Elizabeth snapped his picture as he hopped into his car and drove off. Watching the car leave the parking strip, another thought struck Elizabeth. She sat up straight in the chair.

"Elizabeth, you're really slow today." Mrs. Falcon said she and her husband were home a few days before the hurricane and then left for Maine because of the storm warnings. But, I never saw them. They didn't ask for their mail. They were out of sight, of course, I'm only in front of the house for a minute as I stop at the other mailboxes on the street. That puts Mr. Falcon in Port Orange when Linda Darling was murdered and not in Maine like I assumed.

Elizabeth walked to her car, almost in a trance, not noticing anyone or anything around her. She had to report this new piece of information to her client. She didn't know where Rocket was. The last thing he said was that he was following the money.

Chapter 34

———

JOE RANG THE DOORBELL a second time shifting his feet as he looked up at the seagulls flying over the ocean on the coast of Maine. A woman from inside called out, "I'm coming. I'm coming." The door opened, and a lady with short white hair looked out through the screen at him.

"Sorry, it took me so long. We get so few visitors that I didn't realize it was my doorbell sounding off. What can I do for you?" The lady stayed behind the screen door and did not invite Joe to come inside. After all, he was a stranger.

"I'm sorry to bother you, ma'am. I'm looking for a friend of mine. He doesn't seem to be at home, and he's not answering his telephone. I was wondering if you might happen to know if he's vacationing out of the country."

"We're quite spread out here in Ogunquit. Mind our own business. What's your friend's name?"

"Falcon. Walter and Mona Falcon. They live down the road a piece on the water...not far from here."

"Never heard that name before. But as I said, we mind our own business. Bout the only time we catch up on any gossip is when we go into town. How long they been living here, or do they just come up for the summer months?"

"You're right. I think they only come here late July and August. They live the rest of the time in Florida."

"There you have it...takes awhile to meet people around here. Only one summer, you say. No wonder I haven't heard of them."

"Thanks anyway. Have a nice day."

Joe stopped at a couple more houses but received the same story—everyone pretty much sticks to themselves, especially in the summer trying to avoid the tourists who clog the small shops looking for souvenirs of their Maine vacation. Following the tip the first lady gave him, he drove into the business district—one street, a few blocks long, packed with little shops. The grocery store in Ogunquit was at least a hundred years old. It wouldn't have surprised Joe if the old timer with unruly gray hair standing behind the counter, his overalls covered by a white bib apron, was a wax figure.

"Can I help you, son?"

"Just looking for some snacks for the road," Joe said. "Wish you had something stronger than a Coke. My trip's been a bust."

"Sorry to hear about your trip." The storekeeper shook out a brown-paper bag and started entering Joe's purchases into the antique cash register.

"I was looking for Walter Falcon. You know him? His neighbors don't seem to know anything about him or his wife. I guess their property is pretty remote."

"Sure do. Always buys a little something sweet for his missus."

Doesn't' sound like the Falcon I know. Joe brought a small pack of cheesy snacks to the counter.

"Course, they can't seem to make up their minds this year...going back and forth to Florida. Fact is, they just left here bout two days ago. Old Walt didn't seem too happy this time."

"There goes my phone," Joe said. "Excuse me a minute. I have to step outside. Better reception. Just ring those things up, and I'll be right back."

Joe stepped out and pulled his sunglasses parked on top of his head down over his eyes. The people in Maine were the recipients of a beautiful summer day—crystal blue sky, a slight warm breeze, and a blinding sun.

"Hello, hello."

"Hello, Mr. Rocket. This is Elizabeth, your PI, reporting in."

"Stitch, I know you're my PI. Do you have something for me? I'm rather busy."

"Well, excuse me. I certainly wouldn't want to disturb you with any PI report."

"Stitch, I didn't mean it that way. Please, go ahead. I'm listening."

"Two things. One. A man was parked near the canal, you know, the canal where—"

"Okay, the canal, go on."

"I will if you'll stop interrupting me. This man said he presumed I was the mail lady who was blown into the canal. I said I was. He said he was doing a story on the incident and wondered if I had seen or knew where the man was who helped me that day. I said no and then get this. I asked for his name and to show me his credentials, you know, a reporter's badge."

"Did he show them to you?"

"No. In fact, he jumped in his car and drove off. Joe, he was no reporter."

"What did he look like?"

"Short, bald, slimy."

"Did he give you his name?"

"No. As I said he took off in his car. But, Joe, I think I saw him again."

"Where?"

"About an hour later. Actually a few minutes ago."

"Where are you?"

"I'm in my car outside Panera Bread. I was calling—"

"Stitch, the man, where did you see him?"

"I'm trying to tell you. I was having a soda, answering a few ads in the paper about apartments for rent. I looked up, and he was standing by his car in the parking lot. He looked right at me. I grabbed my phone and took his picture."

"Quick thinking. What did he do, after he saw you looking at him?"

"He got in his car and drove away. Why, Joe? Do you think you know who he is?"

"Maybe. Send me his picture. What's this about an apartment? Are you going to move?"

"Yah. I bought a gun, you know, for protection because this is a murder case and my mother—"

"A gun? Stitch have you ever used a gun?"

"Yes, a few times with my dad. It's okay, Joe. But I appreciate your concern."

"I just don't want anything to happen to my favorite PI."

"Favorite PI. I like the sound of that. Anyway, the apartment thing—mom doesn't want a gun in the house so—"

"Maybe you should wait...to move out. That man may be following you hoping you'll lead him to me. I'd feel better knowing your dad has his eyes out for you."

"Joe, I'm fine, honestly. But that's not all. Number two. I was finishing up my mail run this afternoon, turned the corner onto Red Snapper Lane, and the Falcon's garage door was up. Mrs. Falcon was pulling out what looked like bags of groceries. I made a quick decision to take advantage of this opportunity and grabbed a bunch of circulars."

"Circulars?"

"Yes. As I said to you once before, for a smart stockbroker, you can be very dense. Their mail was still being forwarded to Maine, and the circulars were all I had."

"Keep this up, and I'll have to give you a bonus."

"Normally I would take offense at such a sarcastic crack, but I'm feeling generous today. I talked to her friendly-like, and out of the blue she said the past few weeks had been, just a sec let me look at my notes, 'rather stressful.' She said this third trip back was the last. When I said they were at least lucky to have missed the hurricane, she replied, and this is the big quote, 'we were here just three days when we heard the warnings that a possible hurricane was coming.' She went on to say, and I quote again, 'Walt thought we'd better leave before we were trapped here.'"

"Stitch, *that* is big. Remind me to give you a hug and a kiss on top of that bonus. Anything else?"

"No."

Joe could barely hear her answer. "Elizabeth, are you okay?" He looked at his phone...the line was dead. *How about that she hung up.*

He punched the dial-back button. "Elizabeth, why did you hang up on me?"

"I'm sorry, Joe."

"You could've been mugged. Please don't do that again."

"I promise. Where are you?"

"I'm in Maine, trying to track down some information on Falcon."

"Joe...you be careful, too, you hear? I think we're getting close to solving this murder and you could be in danger."

"I hear you, Stitch. I'll call you when I'm on my way back to Florida...probably tomorrow."

Joe pocketed his cell and walked back into the store to settle up and pay for his purchases. Counting out the bills and change, a question came to his mind.

"You know they had quite a storm rip through Florida a few weeks ago. I hope Walter wasn't caught in it on one of his trips."

"Oh, I remember that. It was one of those rare times when he was out of sorts, surly even. Mrs. Falcon was in the car. She usually comes in with him but not this time. He grabbed a few things off the shelves, some drinks from the cooler, and a few packages from the frozen food section. I remember it clearly because he kept knocking things over. I told him to never mind. I'd pick up the stuff that fell on the floor. He said something like they escaped the storm down south just hours before it hit. He threw a hundred dollar bill at me, yelled to keep the change, and took off down the road."

Chapter 35

———

IT WAS SUNDAY MORNING, and Elizabeth was eager to begin executing the game plan she had laid out the night before. She and Maggie were going to visit the canal. Maybe she had missed something each day as she drove by, looking at the scene, where she and Joe had pulled the body out of the water.

Up, dressed, and on the road a little before sunrise, she made a stop at McDonald's for her favorite latte and two sausage patties in a biscuit for Maggie. Maggie sniffed at the bag, uttered a soft whine from her partially open jaw, her tongue hanging out in anticipation of receiving the juicy treat.

"Just hang on, Mags. Wait until we get to the canal."

Elizabeth, driving to Turtle Grove Estates in the pre-dawn light, couldn't stop her mind from wandering back to her telephone conversation with Joe the day before. *On the one hand,* she thought, *they did their usual sniping back and forth, but what disturbed her was his seemingly genuine concern for her welfare...and her sudden concern for his. What was that all about?* And, whenever he said he might have to give her a hug and a kiss...a kiss? She felt flustered, her breathing stopped momentarily, but her heart raced.

"Maggie, you and I have to watch ourselves around Joe...not be too friendly. After all, he is a client...but I do like it when he calls me Stitch. It's rather sweet, don't you think?"

Maggie gave her a slurp on the cheek, then returned her nose to the slight crack in the window.

Ten minutes later, Maggie received her reward for being patient. Elizabeth sat on the grassy bank of the canal, sipping her latte. Maggie downed the sausage patty in one gulp and trotted off to the bushes.

Elizabeth's eyes scanned every inch of the canal from the culvert to the spot her vehicle had landed, continuing on down to the bushes where Maggie found Joe's shoe and back again. The morning sun, now a little above the horizon, struck the ground at an angle over her shoulder, the beams appearing to be parallel with the grass. The brightness hurt Elizabeth's eyes. She looked away to her right and glanced again at the culvert. Along the top edge of the opening, she detected a reflection, a sparkle of light, as the sun struck the pipe head-on through the dappled opening of the leaves above.

Elizabeth stood up, brushed off the rear of her jeans, and stepped toward to the culvert. Sipping her latte, she knelt on the grass, then laid on her stomach, and inched forward her white T-shirt picking up grass stains. From her angle, now that she was closer to the pipe, the sunlight no longer caught whatever caused the reflection in the first place. Maggie mimicked

every action her mistress took, inching along with her on the bank.

Elizabeth, her coffee cup lying in the grass behind her, was now within five feet of the opening, saw what appeared to be shreds of cloth hanging from the edge of the muddy pipe. "Stay here, Maggie, I'm going to check out those threads."

Elizabeth took off her cherry-red sandals, lined them up on the edge of the canal, and scooted down the bank a couple of feet into the water which was now up to the calves of her legs. "Please, don't let me step on a snake." She looked up to the sky and quickly back to the opening in the culvert.

She took two large strides in the murky water which ran slowly to the other end of the canal, through the drain and out to the river. She leaned over and touched the top of the embankment over the culvert.

"The blanket. Maggie, these are pieces of wool from the blanket."

Maggie, not able to contain herself, jumped into the water to play with her mistress. Paddling, head up, she swam around in circles.

"Maggie, no. You're splashing me. Out. Out."

Elizabeth pivoted to climb out of the muck and stepped on something sharp. "Ouch. Oh, that hurt." She stooped to rub her foot putting her hand in the water. *That's not a stone. What is it?* She pushed her hand deeper. "Oh, my God, it's a gun. Maggie, it's a gun," she said pulling her find from its grave and laying it on the grass. Maggie responded with a half whine, a half bark.

They both clamored out of the canal, Maggie instantly shaking herself, spraying more water on her mistress. Elizabeth didn't seem to notice. She was now soaking wet as she hustled back to where she had given Maggie her sausage patty. Taking out the second McMuffin breakfast sandwich and laying it on the ground in front of the gleeful dog, she put the paper napkins in her pocket and headed back to the culvert with the empty sack. She stood over the gun lying on the grass and pulled out two of the paper napkins carefully wrapping them around the barrel and put the bundle in the bottom of the bag.

Leaving the McMuffin package at the top of the bank, she once again stepped into the muck, giving Maggie stern instructions to stay put, and made her way to the opening of the culvert. Taking out more napkins, she pulled a large pinch of the fibers from the mud-encrusted pipe, wiping her fingers on the open napkin depositing a sample of the material. She performed this task two more times and then carefully folded the napkin. Climbing out of the canal, she placed the packet of fibers in the bag on top of the gun.

Maggie took a few steps into the canal and started drinking the water when a black snake slithered along the grass. Seeing the snake she yelped and ran to the car, ears back, whimpering all the way.

"It's okay, girl," Elizabeth called out to the retreating dog. "I don't like snakes either. Just be glad it wasn't an alligator."

Elizabeth picked up her empty latte cup, scurried to her car, and opened the door. Maggie jumped in as Elizabeth carefully placed the bag and empty cup behind the driver's seat and climbed in after her, both drenched. The yellow coupe took off down the street and disappeared as it rounded the bend in the road.

———

HEARING A COMMOTION OUTSIDE, Walter Falcon jumped out of bed. He quickly stepped to the window, nervously looking out over the street and the canal beyond. Seeing nothing, he relaxed, rubbed his disheveled hair, and ambled to the kitchen to make his morning coffee while he read the Sunday newspaper.

Chapter 36

———

SO THAT WAS IT. His trip was in vain. Joe felt he had all the information he was going to get from his stay in Ogunquit. It was precious little. But he had to make one more stop before driving to Boston to catch a return flight to Florida. He had to check out Falcon's summer home, just in case good old Walter had stashed some papers there for safe keeping.

The long, winding driveway to the house was no better than a dirt road leading to the ocean. Thanks to Elizabeth's call, he knew the Falcons were back in Port Orange so he didn't believe his search would be disturbed. Driving through the pine trees and thick underbrush he knew none of the neighbors would see him, not that they cared. The ones he had spoken with over the past few days didn't even know anyone by the name of Falcon had taken up residence.

It was mid-day, and angry clouds had drifted in off the ocean. The weather report was for rain. Joe could see heavy fog off in the distance. A clearing suddenly appeared at the end of the lonely access road. The Falcon estate sprawled out in front of Joe. "Well, well, Walter, so this is how you spent my money? Very nice indeed."

Joe turned the car around so he'd be headed out and backed up close to the garage. He walked to the back door and tried the knob. It was locked. Pulling a credit card from his wallet, he tried a trick he had learned in prison and gained immediate access to the kitchen. "Walter, I'm going to have to tell you how to keep your houses safe from intruders. It's hard to believe you didn't install a better lock on your door, plus an alert system to the police station."

Wandering around the house, he found a jar of peanuts and helped himself. A can of beer in the refrigerator made a nice happy hour along with the nuts. In what looked like an office or a den, Joe systematically went through the desk drawers and checked the one bookcase to see if he could find another fake box. Turning up nothing, he went back to the living room and pulled the draw drapes back a few feet.

"You sure know how to pick 'em, Walt. This is some view." A small bird flew into the window. Startled, Joe opened the drapes wider and saw the dazed seagull sitting on the grass. Trying to stand on wobbly legs, it took off.

A sharp noise like a door banging shut cut the silence inside the house. Joe stood still, cocking his head to the side, listening. He didn't hear anything further, but the hackles went up on the back of his neck. From his time in prison, several inmates told him if you think you hear something get moving...doesn't matter if it's a cat or a parakeet, draw your weapon and get out.

Softly running down the carpeted hall to the den where he had admired Falcon's gun collection, he entered the room, pulled the knob of the glass door on the case. It was locked, and his credit card trick didn't work. Picking up a small statue of a bull off the desk, he lightly tapped the glass. Small shards fell silently to the carpet. Reaching inside, he released the latch of the door and swung it open. The case contained four rifles anchored to the back and two pistols lying at the bottom. He picked up both pistols putting one in his pants pocket and holding the second in his right hand.

"Hey, Joe, come out, come out wherever you are. You really shouldn't break into people's houses. Breaking and entering seem to be a bad habit of yours. Probably learned it from all those criminals you palled around within prison."

The voice came from the front of the house. Joe quickly left the den, looking right then left before stepping into the hallway. He calculated his quickest escape route was the kitchen door, the way he came in. It was in the back of the house and away from the voice.

He backed down the hallway to the kitchen holding the gun out in front of him with both hands. He didn't know if it was loaded. He could only pray there were bullets in the clip.

"Now, come on, Joe. Let's you and me sit down and have a beer. You've led me on a merry chase, but I knew if I kept following that quirky mail lady, I'd find you. But I didn't expect to hit the bulls-eye so fast after I planted the bug in her car. Of course, old Walter owes me big time for hiring a pilot to fly me here overnight."

"Yah, well you shouldn't have wasted his money." Joe stepped into the doorway of the kitchen and fired at Smitty who was walking through the hall toward him, hitting him in the foot. Smitty yelped, falling to the floor but at the same time pulling the trigger on his gun aimed in Joe's direction.

Joe cried out in pain, dropping his gun and reaching for his shoulder. Spinning around he darted to the kitchen door and ran out to his rental car. Fumbling with the keys, he finally was able to jam the car key into the ignition, gunned the engine, and careened down the road. He had driven less than fifty yards when he spotted a car off to the side between two pine trees. Slamming on the brakes, he pulled out the gun he had put in his pants pocket. He rolled down the window and shot out the two tires on the driver's side of the parked car. Satisfied they were flat, he again pushed the gas pedal to the floor until he reached the main road. He slowed down to the speed limit and was relieved to see a gas station not far ahead. Driving with one hand, he felt his shoulder with the other. His fingers were immediately smeared with blood. He pulled into the gas station, grabbed his duffel bag, and entered the small building.

"Do you have a restroom?" Joe asked.

"Yah, sure," the kid looked apprehensive but took a key off the peg, nodded to his left, indicating the direction of the lavatory.

Once inside the small restroom, Joe locked the door behind him, and carefully removed his bloody shirt. Looking in the mirror, he heaved a sigh of relief.

"Smitty, old boy, that was a lucky shot...for me. Looks like a flesh wound."

Joe relieved himself, then, moving gingerly, he washed his hands and face. Pulling a clean shirt from his bag, he threw the bloody one into the trashcan. Carefully putting on the clean black golf shirt, he wedged a white sock under the sleeve just in case the wound started to bleed again.

Joe closed his bag, opened the restroom door a crack, checking to see if it was all clear. He knew Smitty would not be able to drive his car with flat tires, and Joe was sure he had hit him somewhere below the knee. Seeing nothing suspicious, he dropped off the restroom key to a wide-eyed attendant, climbed into his car and headed for the Boston airport.

Chapter 37

TIMOTHY DARLING WAS DEPRESSED. The insurance company was withholding the payout on his sister's life insurance policy. Her company, which she partnered with Falcon, had deposited her last paycheck into her checking account but it wasn't at all certain that the commissions due her estate would follow anytime soon.

"Lucky I'm a co-signer on her bank accounts," he said to himself. He was alone. He felt abandoned.

Sitting in his favorite chair, a green-leather recliner, he leaned to his right and set the empty beer bottle down on the floor, his second for the morning. Staring out the window at the ducks swimming in the small lake, he pondered his life and what he would do next.

"There's no reason the insurance money won't be paid," he muttered. "The question is when. I'd better be careful with my spending—no more splurges on clothes. Better hold off trading my Corvette for that little Porsche I saw in the window last week. My wallet may feel a pinch, but it shouldn't last long. Should it? I don't think so."

He looked around the living room. It was large with a vaulted ceiling. He smiled at the light green walls...Linda's favorite color, except for black. She always wore black. The house was lonely without his sister. It was filled with that empty feeling.

"Maybe I should get a girlfriend. Knock off the one-night stands. Yah, a live-in relationship. But no marriage. That's the trouble with live-ins. Next thing you know they want you to marry them. Oh, no.

I'm not divvying up any of my payoff money for a divorce. Maybe a live-in isn't such a good idea."

He heard the phone ring in the kitchen.

Timothy pulled the lever letting the footrest down and hauled himself out of the chair.

The phone rang twice more.

He sauntered to the kitchen and picked up the receiver on the fifth ring.

"Hello."

"Timothy?"

"Yah, oh, hi."

"Where were you? I almost hung up."

"I was busy."

"How're you holding up?"

"Fine. Fine. No problem."

"Good. You must remain strong."

"I am. Are you insinuating I'm not?"

"No. It's just a feeling I have that we're going to be tested."

"No problem here. Worry about yourself. I just wish the insurance check would come through."

"That probably won't happen until the medical examiner releases her body."

"That's what I figure," Timothy said, swiping another beer from the refrigerator, screwing off the cap, and taking a long swallow.

"You must remain strong."

"So you said."

"And, don't drink too much."

"Yah, yah. You can count on me."

Chapter 38

——

"STITCH, WHERE ARE YOU? What's that noise?"

"I'm at a gas station. Are you alright? You sound tired." Elizabeth, one hand pumping gas into the tank, the other holding the phone to her ear, started shaking when she heard Joe's voice. Maggie's head poked out through the open window, looking from the clicking of the gas pump to her mistress at the rear of the car.

"Something happened this morning. I want you off the case," he said.

"What happened? Are you sure you're okay?"

"Yes, but this is getting too dangerous. I'm afraid you may get hurt."

"Joe, I know being a PI won't be a stroll on the beach. Even if you fire me, I'm still going to investigate what happened to Linda, and hopefully remove you from the person-of-interest list."

The bell sounded on the gas pump, and Elizabeth returned the nozzle to the holder. Still hanging onto the phone, she swiped her credit card, entered her zip code.

"Joe...are you there?" After screwing on the gas cap, she climbed into her car. "Joe?"

"Yes, I'm here."

"Listen, I was about to call you. I have some new information, important information. Where are you?"

"Can you step out of your car?"

"Yes, but why?"

"Are you outside your car? Walk away a few yards."

"Okay, I'm away from the car. I asked you where you're calling from."

"I'm in Boston, at Logan Airport. My flight is scheduled to land in Orlando at three something, and then I'll drive to Port Orange. Do you know where Stonewood is, on Dunlawton, the bar?"

"Sure...south side."

"Let's meet there at six-thirty unless you hear from me before, and be sure you aren't followed. Do you know how to lose a tail?"

"My friend, driving evasively is taught in PI 101." Elizabeth said looking over at Maggie, her nose out the window again.

"Your yellow car makes you stand out like a sitting duck. You might as well have a beacon on top and a megaphone blasting, 'I'm over here. Come and get me.'"

"Joe, I don't know what happened, but something is bothering you. I'll see you at six-thirty."

"Right. Promise me you'll stay alert."

"I promise."

"And, when you're in your car don't talk to anyone. I'll explain when I see you. Gotta run."

The line went dead.

Fifteen minutes later Elizabeth was in her bedroom composing her report as Maggie slept fitfully on the bed. The McDonald's bag was lying on the desk beside her monitor. Elizabeth, fingers hovering over the keyboard, looked at her furry friend. *Poor dog. She's probably dreaming about black snakes.*

Elizabeth looked back at her monitor. "The fibers are probably from the blanket Linda was wrapped in, and they prove she was definitely inside the pipe. But, more important, who dropped the gun into the canal?" She stared at the sack, the contents in her mind's eye.

"Who killed Linda Darling?" She continued to stare at her report displayed on the screen at the same time tapping her pen on the pad of paper containing her notes.

"Falcon? Living across the street, it wouldn't be that difficult to stuff her body in the culvert. I can't believe Joe killed her. His gripe is with Falcon even though he did show up at exactly the moment the body floated into my truck. And, Miss PI, don't forget dear Timothy Darling. He certainly has a motive—all that insurance money. No, he's too wimpy. I can't see him putting a bullet into his sister's chest."

Chapter 39

——

THE BAR WAS DARK. It took Elizabeth a few seconds to adjust her eyes from the bright sun.

"May I show you a table in the dining room, miss?"

"No thanks. I'm meeting a gentleman," Elizabeth said searching for Joe.

"Ah, a gentleman did say he was expecting a lady. Come with me."

Elizabeth followed the hostess to a booth tucked into the back corner, the darkest part of the bar. The only illumination came from a small votive on the table, a few spotlights over the bar, and a couple of television sets anchored to the ceiling broadcasting a Jaguar pre-season game against the Patriots. Joe stood up to greet Elizabeth as she slid onto the bench facing him across the lacquered table.

Neither said a word as they searched each other's face, lingering a few moments. Elizabeth stunned at the intensity she saw in Joe's eyes, quickly looked away.

Joe leaned back on the bench but was unable to pull his eyes away from the woman sitting across from him. He unbuttoned his jacket and signaled to the waiter.

"I'll have another scotch on the rocks, please. What would you like, Elizabeth?"

"That sounds good."

"Stitch, you can have whatever you want. This is a stiff drink. I've been on the road for three days—"

"What, Mr. Rocket? You don't think I can handle it?"

Joe nodded to the bartender to bring what the lady ordered. "And please bring us a couple of orders of your tomato bruschetta with mozzarella and one of those marinated mushroom dishes."

"Very good, Mr. Rocket."

Elizabeth's eyebrows went up. "Is this one of your haunts?"

"Used to be. After tonight I won't dare come here again...at least for awhile."

"Why are you staring at me?"

"You're dressed...well, differently than I've seen you before. Your wardrobe is very colorful, but this black dress..."

Elizabeth smiled. She wasn't going to admit how many outfits she had slipped over her head getting ready to meet him while Maggie lay on the bed, head between her paws, watching her mistress as the clothes piled up on the floor. Elizabeth would pause taking stock of how she looked in her full-length mirror...one dress after the other.

"I just thought meeting a gentleman for a drink called for something a little less...a little less colorful."

"You look very nice."

"Thanks. You look very...very gentlemanly yourself. It's the first time I've seen you in a suit...quite stockbrokerish." They both laughed letting the awkward moment melt away.

Elizabeth reached to her side and pulled open her black tote.

"I can't see a thing in this light, or non-light." She felt around and pulled out a yellow-lined pad and a black-leather folder. Still searching in the caverns of her tote, Elizabeth finally found what she was looking for, a pencil and a pen. She put the yellow pad on her right side of the table with the pencil on top and pushed the black folder to her left with the pen.

The waiter returned, setting their drinks on the table along with a bowl of peanuts in the center of Elizabeth's desk setup.

Picking up her drink, she raised her glass to Joe's. "Cheers."

"Cheers. Here's to catching the bastard," he said.

"Agree. Here's to catching the bastard, whoever he may be."

Again their eyes locked over the edges of their highball glasses. Joe took a sip of his drink, put the glass back on the table, the movement causing him to wince when his jacket pulled on his wound.

"Joe, you're hurt." Elizabeth's hands flew to surround his fingers holding the glass. "I knew you were hiding something from me."

"I didn't want to tell you over the phone yesterday that I was shot."

"Shot? Where?"

"It's just a flesh wound, my shoulder," he said. His hand lightly touched the area that was tender.

"Did you see a doctor?"

"No. It's really nothing. I picked up some bandages and antiseptic at the drugstore."

"Really, now. You can be so exasperating. An open wound can get infected. How did it happen and who shot you?"

"First of all, it's not open, the bleeding stopped. Second, as to who shot me, you know that guy who told you he was a reporter?"

"Yes, and then I saw him standing in the Panera Bread parking lot, and I sent you his picture."

"That's him. Great picture by the way. His name is Smitty. He's a buddy of Falcon's. I never trusted the guy. Anyway, he cornered me in Falcon's house in Maine, and you'll never guess how he found me."

"How?" Elizabeth took a sip of her drink, riveted on Joe's story.

"He bugged your car?"

"My car?"

"Yah, he confessed he did it. Probably when you caught him standing next to it. He heard our

conversation...when I told you where I was."

"Oh, Joe. We have to find that bug?"

"I know. I'll help you. It's amazing all the little things you pick up in prison—some of it's even useful. Of course, now that we know about it, we could leave it where it is and use it to our advantage, throw him off if we need to." Joe slid his thumb over her fingers. *Why haven't I noticed those beautiful, full ruby lips before? ...and those big brown eyes."*

Elizabeth, realizing she still had her fingers around Joe's hand, and the movement of his thumb over her knuckle sending a jolt through her chest, withdrew her hands to her lap.

Joe smiled and leaned forward in his seat careful not to apply any pressure on his shoulder. "Now, Miss Stitchway, with your desk all set, it looks like you're ready for business. What's this new information you said you had for me?"

"Well, Maggie and I went to the canal early Sunday morning. The sun was just over the horizon."

"Look, I don't care where the sun was."

"Oh, but you should, because without that little fact I may not have seen it."

"Stitch, what is it you saw?" Joe smiled enjoying the exchange with the other side of the table.

"The fibers from the blanket and a gun."

"What? In the canal?"

"Yup. I first saw something glinting in the sunlight on the top edge of the culvert, so I waded in. The water was only about a foot deep in the center, nothing like during the hurricane. Here, let me show you." Elizabeth pulled out the McDonald's bag and retrieved one of the folded napkins. "Now you tell me if that isn't from that Turkish blanket?"

Joe picked up the napkin and went to the bar to get a good look under a spotlight. Returning to the table, he carefully refolded the napkin and handed it back to Elizabeth.

"Well, what do you think? From the blanket?" Elizabeth asked.

"Definitely. What else do you have in that McMuffin bag?"

"I can't take it out here. Just peek inside." Elizabeth pushed the bag over to Joe. He was about to open it when the waiter arrived with their bruschetta and mushrooms. He looked askance at the McDonalds' bag.

"No, no, Jack. Just some pictures my girlfriend wanted to show me."

Jack smiled at Elizabeth and placed the appetizers on the table in a row between them and the obvious business paraphernalia she had laid out.

"Can you get me a refill? Elizabeth, would you like another drink?"

"No. Thanks anyway."

Jack retreated, and Joe once again pulled the bag closer and looked inside. He lifted his eyes to Elizabeth. "Nice work, Stitchway. This was in the canal?"

"I stepped on it. It hurt like the devil."

Joe leaned forward and grasped her hand. "You've come up with some real evidence."

Heat rose in Elizabeth's cheeks. She looked down at his hand and slowly withdrew hers, Impulses darting throughout her body. Not realizing she hadn't breathed since he touched her hand, she inhaled a deep breath of air.

"This is terrific." Joe stood, walked down the length of the bar and back, pounding his fist into his palm. Wincing, he slid back onto the bench and drained his drink, just as Jack set down the refill.

"Stitch, we can't rely on there being any fingerprints on the gun, but maybe we can make Falcon think there are. I have to confront him."

"Joe—" Elizabeth tried to ignore that he was holding her hand again, but then he pushed the plates away and grasped her other hand, staring into her eyes. He continued to stare as if seeing her for the first time. He carefully put her hands down on the table and leaned back.

Her breathing ragged, Elizabeth tried again to speak. "Joe, if you confront Falcon you need to wear a wire or some kind of a recorder...and you should probably be armed. Falcon's killed once. He could just as easily want to dispose of you thinking he'd finally be clear of both of his problems...you and Linda."

"So, you agree with me...you think Falcon killed her."

"Well, isn't this a cozy little twosome." A man tilted toward their booth, placed his drink and then both hands on the table. "Miss Goody Two Shoes and Mr. Money Bags."

Elizabeth recoiled at the smell of Timothy Darling's breath.

"Hello, Tim." Joe rose from the bench and firmly grasped the front of Darling's white golf shirt with his left hand backing him away from the table. "The lady and I are having a nice conversation. Now you go back to the hole you crawled out of."

"Is this man bothering you, Mr. Rocket?" Jack and another waiter appeared on either side of Darling and firmly grasped his arms. Joe released his grip as the two waiters lifted and turned Darling away from the booth.

"You've had enough, Mr. Darling. Let's take you back to the dining room for some coffee before you go home."

"But, but—I'm calling the police," Timothy yelled over his shoulder. "I'm sure they'll be glad to know you're here and with...with her."

"Sorry, Stitch." Joe slid back into the booth.

"Do you think he drinks like that a lot?" Elizabeth asked.

"I honestly don't know, but he sure is drunk tonight."

"Joe, back to what you asked before Timothy came over. Yes. I think Falcon murdered Linda. Of course, with Smitty trying to kill you, maybe Falcon hired him to shoot Linda."

"I thought of that, but even so, Falcon would be guilty of planning it."

"As far as confronting Falcon, I think we should bring the evidence we have to Detective
Armstrong."

"Stitch, I can't go to the police yet. They would hold me in jail until they're convinced I wasn't involved."

"I suppose you're right. I'll talk to Armstrong and the only way I'll give him my evidence is if he agrees that we all cooperate."

"It's worth a try. After all, Smitty did try to kill me."

"I'll talk to Armstrong tomorrow morning...take a sick day."

"Let's get out of here," Joe said. "I'm suddenly feeling very claustrophobic. Darling could have made good on his threat to call the police."

Joe paid the bill while Elizabeth packed up her desk. He escorted her out of the bar and over to her car. "Stitch, I meant what I said on the phone. I'm worried you're going to get hurt."

"I'll be okay, Mr. Rocket. Don't forget you were the one who was shot, not me."

Elizabeth looked up into Joe's dark blue eyes, a smile spreading across her face. "I'll call you after I see Armstrong tomorrow. You know, with my report."

Joe lifted her chin slightly. He bent his head down and gently brushed his lips over hers. Lifting his head, he looked into her large soft eyes. "Be careful, Stitch. I don't want anything to happen to my PI."

Chapter 40

———

"WHERE THE HELL are you, Smitty?" Falcon kept his voice low as he stalked around his office, the plush green carpet silencing his heavy footsteps. Teeth clenched, he squeezed his cell phone in an iron grip. He had left the office door ajar so it would look like business as usual but was careful that Mr. Scott in the adjoining office didn't hear what he was saying. The cleaning kid came in, picked up the wastebasket and left.

"I'm still in Maine. I had a little mishap with our friend Rocket. Did you know he broke into your house up here?"

"Maine? You followed him to Maine?"

"Yeah, I had a tip."

"Shit, I was going to install an alarm system this summer, but with everything that's happening, I forgot. Did he trash the place?"

"No, except for your gun cabinet. He broke the glass and stole at least one gun that I know of."

"So, now the bastard's armed." Falcon hissed.

"Oh, yah. Shot out two of my tires on the rental car, but before that, he shot yours truly in the big toe."

"Tough shit. What about Rocket—did you get him?"

The cleaning kid returned the empty wastebasket, raised his hand in a quiet salute to Falcon and scurried out of the office, continuing his chore of wiping down the baseboards in the hallway.

"I winged him. Not sure how bad he's hurt, but my toe is really throbbing. I'm on crutches."

"Great, the man I hire for a job can't hit the broadside of a barn, and now he's gimpy as well." Falcon rubbed his head.

"Thanks for the sympathy. Oh, and you'll be getting my bill for the plane I chartered."

"Smitty, you're really pushing your luck. Not only didn't you finish the guy but now you're sticking me with the cost of a plane, an expense I might add was for nothing. You boob. I should never have hired a guy with as many screw-ups on his record as you have." Falcon flopped onto his desk chair, bent over and slapped an imaginary speck of dust from his wing-tipped shoe.

"Well, I do have some tidbits of information for you."

"Like what?"

"Like that mail lady of yours is helping Rocket. I bugged her car. Not long after I was rewarded for my efforts. She talked to Rocket. Told him about this man she saw."

"What man...you're not making any sense."

"Me, shithead. She's a smart cookie...figured out I was tailing her. Rocket knew right away it was me from her description."

"So, you're burned by a mail lady. She may be smart, but you're stupid. That certainly cancels any further payments you may have been dreaming about. Don't bother coming around here anymore."

"Not so fast, Walter. We both have some unfinished business. If you think I'm letting this guy get away with blasting my toe, you'd better think again."

Chapter 41

———

THE BOOKING SERGEANT was trying to maintain order. Petty theft, rabble-rousing, and some fistfights were the charges this morning. Perpetrators were being fingerprinted, photographed, and escorted into holding cells. Some were there to spend a few hours cooling off. Armstrong had interrogated others who had committed more serious crimes, such as breaking and entering.

He was writing up his reports when the phone rang on his desk. He sighed as he mechanically pushed the button for line one holding the receiver to his ear with his shoulder.

"Whatcha got, Muriel?" Armstrong gazed at the fabric covering the five-foot-high panels around his office, scanning the notes held in place by different colored pushpins.

"A man, no, sounds more like a kid, is on the line. He asked for you," Muriel said.

"Okay. What's his name?"

"Larry Richards."

"Put him through." The phone now had the detective's full attention.

"Detective Armstrong?"

"Yes, Larry. Nice to hear from you. Is this an invitation to go surfing or do you have something for me?"

"I think I do...have some information. This morning I went to work at F&D to pick up some cleaning hours, on the clock. Every little bit helps the wallet you know."

"Yes, I know, Larry. Go on."

"I overheard Mr. Falcon talking to someone on the phone. He was furious."

"Where are you, Larry?"

"Oh, don't worry, Detective. I'm out in the parking lot. I'm using my cell."

"What did you hear, son?"

"Well, Mr. Falcon was in his office...I wasn't eavesdropping you understand. It just happened that I was outside his office door which was slightly open mind you."

"It's okay, Larry, I get the picture."

"Hang on, let me get my notes so I can tell you exactly what I heard."

Great another wannabe PI, Armstrong thought, tapping his pen on the desk calendar which was full of colorful doodles only Armstrong would be able to decode.

"Here it is. He called the guy he was talking to Smitty, at least I guess it was a man. From what Mr. Falcon said it sounded as if the man was in Maine, Mr. Falcon's house in Maine."

"Go on. What else?

"Mr. Falcon mentioned the name Rocket. I know he had a business partner by that name. Maybe it was him. Anyway, Mr. Falcon asked if he trashed the place and then added that Rocket was armed. Understand, Detective, my notes are all chopped up. I wrote them down as fast as I could in my car before I called you."

"I understand, Larry, continue."

"He said that he couldn't hit the broadside of a barn. I think he was referring to that Smitty on the phone, and that he didn't finish the guy. That sounds really bad don't you think, Detective? The 'didn't finish the guy.' Then he said something about a smart lady. Don't know how that fits, don't know how any of it fits, but it all sounds bad. Oh, and one last thing. Mr. Falcon said that the person on the phone wasn't going to get any further payments."

"It is a puzzle, young man."

"Wait, here's another page. Quote, 'Smitty, you're really pushing your luck. Not only didn't you finish the guy...' I couldn't remember the rest of the sentence. But I have more. Quote, 'So, you're burned by a mail lady' dot dot dot—sorry, I can't read my writing. What do you think, Detective? Helpful?"

"Yes, it is, Larry. More information like this and I'll have to deputize you. Let me know if anything else comes over the transom."

"The what?"

"An old joke."

"Oops, I gotta go. I see Falcon coming...he's heading for his car."

Armstrong put the receiver back in the cradle. His phone immediately rang again.

"Detective, there's a Miss Stitchway on line two. She says it's urge—"

"Elizabeth, are you there?"

"Yes, Detective Armstrong. I have to see you right away."

"Come on over to the department. I'll tell the desk sergeant to bring you straight up to my office."

Chapter 42

——

"THIS IS QUITE A REPORT, Elizabeth. You've been busy. Finding these fibers and the gun is some good work. You've given me a bit of a black eye."

"Thanks, Detective."

"The picture you took with your cell phone of this bald guy. You say his name is Smitty. Do you know his full name?"

"No, and Mr. Rocket has only referred to him as Smitty."

"Ah, yes, the elusive Mr. Rocket. You've given me a report of your findings, plus I see you list three names, possible suspects, for Linda Darling's murder."

Armstrong pushed his glasses up on his nose. "Mr. Falcon—most likely. Mr. Rocket—most unlikely. Mr. Darling—a real dark horse. Too wimpy to shoot put a bullet in his sister's chest."

"That's right. Now, here's what—"

Armstrong raised his hand stopping her in mid-sentence. "Please, Elizabeth. I know you're in contact with Rocket, but I—"

"With all due respect Detective, my client, Mr. Rocket is prepared to cooperate fully with you. But, I'm sure you understand his position he's—"

"He's afraid I'd hold him for questioning. Just out of prison, his position *is* tenuous," Armstrong said looking over the rim of his glasses as they slid down his nose.

"That's right, but we do have a plan, a sting if you will." Elizabeth, sitting ramrod straight in the chair, leaned forward. She whispered,

"My client thinks he can get Falcon to confess, but to make it stick, he wants you to be in on it."

"Mr. Rocket is asking me to help him? That's a bit of a switch don't you think, Elizabeth?" Armstrong said in a whisper leaning closer to her.

"Detective, we don't have a lot of time to discuss this. That Smitty person is on the hunt for my client, which means Mr. Falcon is also gunning for him, and my client believes that Smitty is probably tailing me as well. Smitty could be in your parking lot right now. But, Detective, we do have this plan."

"Yes, your plan." Armstrong leaned back in his chair breaking their conspiratorial position. "Elizabeth, please enlighten me. What is your plan?"

"My client is willing to risk his life by confronting Mr. Falcon." Elizabeth continued to lean and continued to whisper. She abruptly stood up, looked over the partition, checking to see if anyone was there who might overhear their conversation. Satisfied the adjoining cubicle was empty, she sat back down but continued to lean toward Armstrong.

"How is that going to help?" Armstrong inched toward Elizabeth.

"You're going to wire him up," she said in a hushed tone.

"Now how am I going to 'wire him up' if I can't meet with your client?" Armstrong whispered.

"Well, that's it, sir. We're looking for a quid pro quo, you know, we—"

"I'm familiar with the term. When does your client want to confront Mr. Falcon?" Armstrong asked bending further listening intently to what Elizabeth was saying.

"Oh, as soon as possible. As I said, we don't know where Smitty is."

"Elizabeth, you've been very upfront with me. I'm inclined to go along with your...your plan. I'll give the gun and the fibers to our forensics people for analysis. How soon can I meet with Mr. Rocket?" Armstrong stood and looked over the partition, mimicking Elizabeth's movements.

"How about in forty-five minutes?"

"Okay by me."

"Hang on, Detective." Elizabeth flipped open her cell phone and punched Joe's code.

"Hello, Mr. Rocket. I'm sitting here with Detective Armstrong, and he has agreed with our plan. He wants to meet with you, say in forty-five minutes at our pre-arranged location. Is this agreeable with you? ...good."

Elizabeth closed her cell and looked at Armstrong.

"It's a deal, Detective."

"Where?"

"Spruce Creek Recreation Center. Take the nature trail to a narrow bridge. We'll be on the other side. And Detective, drive one of your squad cars, you know, the kind with Port Orange Police in big letters on the side. If Smitty is around that should scare him off."

———

ELIZABETH PARKED IN THE recreation center parking lot and strolled down the nature trail to meet Joe. Seeing him on the other side of the bridge, her bright red lips parted in a smile. Joe walked up to her and wrapped her in a hug. Hesitating only a moment, she returned his hug.

Leaning back on his heels, Joe looked at her and planted a quick kiss on her ruby lips. "You were terrific with the detective, Stitch."

Two shots rang out just missing Joe's head. He looked up over Elizabeth's shoulder and saw Smitty, a boot on his foot protecting his shattered toe, running with a limpy gait toward them. Joe grabbed Elizabeth's hand and tugged her along down the path away from Smitty.

"Come on. We're getting out of here."

They ran along the path, startled birds screeching, frantically flying out of the trees to safety. The trail zigzagged through the thick bushes under the towering old oak and pine trees.

Another shot rang out but was way wide.

"My motorcycle is just ahead."

"But, my car."

"We'll get it later. Come on. We have to keep going."

Joe's motorcycle was locked next to the bicycle rack. He pulled out his keys and quickly straddled the seat. He gave Elizabeth a hand as she swung her leg over the small cushion behind him. Two quick pumps and the bike roared out of the park.

"What about Detective Armstrong?" Elizabeth yelled into Joe's ear.

"Call him. Change the location to...to behind Wal-Mart."

"I can't call and hang onto you at the same time."

Chapter 43

———

THE LATE AFTERNOON SUN beat down on Port Orange. Joe and Elizabeth found some shade under a tree on the back edge of Wal-Mart's receiving dock. Neither said a word as they waited for Detective Armstrong's squad car. They were relieved they had escaped Smitty's gunfire. It had been a close call.

Elizabeth stole a sideways glance at Joe. He had kissed her, and she liked it brief as it was.

"Stitch, you could have been killed. That thug had you in his sights." Joe was leaning against the oak tree looking at Elizabeth.

"Let's not play what if. We survived, and that's all that matters. Once we put our plan into action, he won't get another chance."

"Stitch...I've never met a woman like you. You're tough as nails on the outside and soft as a marshmallow inside—all wrapped up in a rainbow of bright colors."

Shading her eyes with her hand, Elizabeth looked over at Joe's face. She saw kindness and something more...tenderness. Her heart skipped a beat. She quickly looked away. *Focus, Elizabeth. Focus.*

They both squinted into the sun as they saw a squad car rounding the corner of the store. It coasted to a stop in front of them. Armstrong slid out of his vehicle and joined the pair sitting on a bed of leaves under the tree. Joe stood as the officer approached.

"Mr. Rocket, I presume?" With a friendly smile, Armstrong extended his hand to Joe.

"Glad to meet you, Detective. Sorry, we had to change the location of our visit. Seems we suddenly had an unwanted guest."

"Smitty found us," Elizabeth said. "I told you he was following me."

"Miss Stitchway, if I may make a recommendation. Your car—"

"I know. Change the color." Elizabeth looked at Joe, eyebrows raised, daring him to make a comment. He shrugged his shoulders but grinned in acknowledgement that he had told her the same thing.

"Mr. Rocket, this PI of yours has built a compelling scenario fingering Mr. Falcon as a killer. I'd like to know how you see it."

"She's spot on. Together, I believe we can give you enough evidence for an arrest."

"Yes, well, we'll see. I read the transcripts of your trial. The evidence made it quite clear that you embezzled money from your partners, Mr. Falcon and Miss Darling." Armstrong slapped his wrist, flicked the dead mosquito away. "I was particularly interested in what you had to say, or I guess yelled out, after the announcement of the verdict. I believe you said, 'I'll get you.' I also called the prison where you were incarcerated. The Warden said you were a model prisoner, but he also thought you were full of anger and living for the time when you could extract revenge on your partners. Is that true?"

"I'm not going to deny I want revenge. But over the last few weeks, I've come to the realization it would be wise to channel those feelings through the law. However, I still long for the day when I see Falcon hauled into court in shackles."

"I'm glad to hear that, the law part." Armstrong stretched out brushing some leaves off of his pant leg.

Joe glanced at Elizabeth, her soft brown eyes and red lips smiling back at him.

Armstrong sat up straight. "Now, let's hear about this plan. By the way, when I turned into the recreation park, a black car was leaving, going rather fast."

"It could have been Smitty," Elizabeth said. "His car is black. Joe, why don't you start laying out our plan for the detective?"

Unable to control his energy, Joe stood up, walked forward a few steps, then back to Armstrong. Sitting on his haunches, looking into Armstrong's eyes, he began to reveal their plan.

"Falcon has a quick temper especially if he thinks he's being challenged. I found evidence in his house proving he and Linda cooked the books, making it look like I embezzled funds from their clients and the two of them when it was really the other way around."

"Where is this evidence now?" Armstrong asked.

"In the attic over Falcon's garage. He hid a box of documents showing the amount and where each chunk of money was transferred."

"How long ago did you see these papers?"

"Almost four weeks. He's been in Maine most of that time. He and Mona returned last Friday. I'm sure he feels the box is safe."

"Why would he keep such incriminating evidence?"

"Oh, that's easy." Joe stood. Looked off into the distance. "In his mind, with me sitting in prison, he could turn the tables on Linda. I think she figured out his scheme, and that he wasn't going to marry her, so she threatened him, and he killed her to shut her up for good." Joe looked back at Elizabeth and sat down cross-legged beside her.

"I see. It does sound plausible," Armstrong said.

"I found another piece of evidence for you, Detective." Joe pulled the Velcro away from the change pocket in his shorts. He dug around and pulled out a bullet. "I found this in the box spring in the master bedroom. My guess is he shot her in his bed, wrapped her in the blanket, stuffed her in the culvert across the street from the house. I bet it matches the gun Stitch, err Elizabeth found in the canal, and the fibers I'm sure will match the blanket over the couch in the living room."

Elizabeth stood up, swatted leaves off the seat of her lime-green shorts, and stomped down the slope to Joe's bike. She turned back to the two men her lips shut tight, eyes piercing, brows furrowed, and her arms crossed over her chest. She took a few steps, abruptly turned and picked up her candy-striped tote off the back of the motorcycle. She charged back to where the men were sitting.

Armstrong looked at her. "What's the matter, Elizabeth?"

"Oh, nothing, Nothing at all. So glad that Mr. Rocket shared this piece of evidence with you. Of course, his PI wouldn't be interested in knowing about this bullet would she? Just how long have you had this little trinket, Mr. Rocket?"

"Stitch, I—"

"Let's get on with the plan unless you have something else you want to show the detective."

"No, I—"

"Okay, you guys. You can settle this, whatever this is, later. Mr. Rocket—"

"Joe, make it Joe." He was now glaring back at Elizabeth.

"Yes, Joe. When do you want to confront Mr. Falcon?" Armstrong asked.

"Tomorrow. His house. Three o'clock."

"Very well," the detective said. "You're going to have to come into the department to get the wire and test it's working properly, say in an hour?"

"An hour works."

"Detective Armstrong, can you give me a lift to my car?" Elizabeth asked as she stomped down to the pavement.

Chapter 44

———

THERE WAS NO CHITCHAT at the Stitchway dinner table. Elizabeth, head down, pushed the peas around her plate and remained unresponsive to her parents' efforts to draw her into their conversation. Dinner was usually full of animated chatter. Harry and Martha enjoyed hearing about their daughter's encounters with her clients while she was depositing the day's mail. Tonight was different.

"Sorry, Mom. I'm not very hungry—" The ringing of Elizabeth's cell interrupted her. She dug out her phone, checking the caller ID. She immediately left the table and walked into the living room.

"Hello, Joe."

"Stitch, I'm outside. Please come out. Please talk to me."

Elizabeth closed her cell. "Rocket's outside. I'll be right back."

She quickly walked to the screen door and pushed it open. Joe was leaning against her car, cell phone still in his hand, looking at the blank display.

"Joe..."

"Stitch, please let me explain. Today—"

Elizabeth sauntered up to him and touched the WF monogram on his shirt pocket, a shirt he had borrowed from Falcon's closet.

"Stop," she whispered. "I acted like a school girl. You're fighting to get your life back, and I want to help you do that. I have complete trust in you. Do you believe me?"

"Yes, oh, yes. I don't know why I didn't tell you about the bullet. I do trust you...and—"

Elizabeth slowly traced his lips with her finger. Joe grasped her hand, kissed her palm, took her in his arms and tenderly kissed her lips. She leaned into him, his warmth flowing through them both as his kiss deepened.

Elizabeth slowly, reluctantly, pulled back but remained in his arms. "Promise me you'll be careful tomorrow," she said.

"I promise." He bent down and kissed her again, holding her against him.

Slowly moving out of his embrace, she asked, "Did you see Armstrong?"

"Yes, we're all set. He, as well as his officers, will hear and record everything. I changed the time to nine in the morning. I want to be sure Falcon's home. He never leaves for work before ten."

Elizabeth fished in her shorts pocket and pulled out a small wafer, the size of a thin dime. "Put this in your shirt pocket tomorrow. It's a bug. I'll hear you talking to Falcon, monitoring what's going on. I know Armstrong outfitted you with a sophisticated device, but I want to hear what's going on, too. I'll be by the canal until I hear you start talking to Falcon and then I'll park by the mailbox."

"Stitch, you're such a breath of fresh air. I care about—"

"Well, aren't you just the chatterbox, but hold that thought...we'll pick it up tomorrow night. As of now, you have a dinner invitation to meet my mom and dad. Do you think you can make it?"

"A family of alligators couldn't stop me. I'd better get going before Smitty gets the bright idea of looking for me here."

Joe kissed her quickly and climbed onto his bike. "See you tomorrow for dinner if not before."

Chapter 45

———

IS THIS WHAT LOVE FEELS LIKE? For the first time in his life, Joe had someone he cared for, to live for. His parents were born during the great depression. His father became a banker and trained Joe to revere the almighty dollar. His mother was of the same mind as his father. Her voice still rang in his ears. "No amount of money is ever enough," she told him. "In the end, money is the only thing that matters." He could hear them bickering over spending one dollar let alone thousands.

"You were wrong," he yelled at the top of his lungs over the roar of his motorcycle. "Elizabeth is more important, and God have mercy on anyone who hurts her."

He pulled under the carport of the trailer home he was renting on Rose Bay. Once inside, he stripped down, carefully removing the wafer Elizabeth had given him as well as the device in his pants pocket that Armstrong had checked out earlier.

Joe took a long shower—a refinement of tomorrow's plan developing in his mind. He smiled at the thought of a plan—a favorite word of Elizabeth's. After drying off, he laid out his clothes on the living room couch—long sleeve cotton dress shirt, cargo pants, belt, socks, and shoes—all black.

Satisfied with his selection, he set his alarm clock for 2:00 a.m.—four hours away. He stretched out on his bed. He knew sleep would elude him, but at least he'd get some rest.

Time passed slowly. Restless, Joe rolled over in bed, reached out and shut off the alarm before it rang. He dressed and fixed a cup of coffee. While it was perking, he placed Armstrong's device in his right shirt pocket, and Elizabeth's in his left, over his heart. He followed the advice of an inmate who admonished him to never go into battle without a gun, a tiny screwdriver for picking locks, duct tape, and some lengths of rope.

He checked the handgun from Falcon's gun case. There were three bullets left in the clip after he shot out Smitty's tires. Stuffing the gun into one of the pants pockets, he filled two others with a small leftover roll of duct tape and two short bungee cords. Looking out the kitchen window into the night, he again went over his preparations. He drank his coffee and put the empty cup in the sink.

"Time to go, Joe, old boy. You've been dreaming of this day for a long time—let's just pray you can pull it off. You have a very important lady waiting on the other side. Don't you dare disappoint her."

Fifteen minutes later, in the warm night air, he quietly walked his bike into the clubhouse

parking lot of Turtle Grove Estates. After chaining it to the end of the bicycle rack, he set out on foot to Falcon's house. Instead of going by the canal, he maneuvered down Red Snapper Lane on the blind side of the house. He planned to enter the garage through the side door from the garden. Removing the small screwdriver to pick the lock, he found the knob turned in his hand. The door wasn't locked.

"Not so fast, shithead. You and I have some unfinished business," Smitty said poking a gun into Joe's ribs. "Back up, nice and easy. You and I are going to take a little drive."

Joe did as he was told, but he suddenly twisted around slamming his heel down onto Smitty's wounded toe. Smitty cried out in pain dropping his weapon. Joe pushed him face down on the grass so he couldn't cry out again. Reaching into his pocket for the bungee cord he tried in vain to tie Smitty's legs together. Smitty was kicking violently making it impossible to hold him down and secure the cord at the same time.

"Here, let me help you with that."

"Gus, where did you come from?"

"Shut up, brother, and put a knot in that damn toy rope." Gus pushed Smitty's face into the ground. "Get the bastard's wrists, will ya, Joe? I don't have all night."

Joe flashed a smile at his former cellmate and quickly tied Smitty's wrists behind his back, his cries of pain muffled in the grass. Joe tore off a piece of duct tape as Gus grabbed Smitty by the hair to lift his head. Joe slapped the tape over Smitty's mouth.

"Do you have another little rubber band for this creeps feet?" Gus asked.

"Yah, right here."

Gus wound the second cord around Smitty's ankles and dragged him into the bushes along the property line about twenty-five feet from the garage. "I don't know what you're planning, Joe, but it looks like fun. I'll wait around, out of sight, in case you need me."

Before Joe could reply Gus was gone. He took a deep breath. The door into the garage remained ajar. He had one more errand to make plus a call to Elizabeth before taking up his position.

Satisfied he had taken care of everything he planned to do, Joe climbed up into the attic for the last time. He leaned back against a rafter, wiped the sweat from his face, and began his vigil—waiting for nine o'clock. The stage was set.

———

INSIDE THE HOUSE, Walter sat up in bed. He went to his bedroom window and peered out across the street to the canal. There was a slight rattle in the vents as the air conditioner switched on. "Must have been an animal. My mind's starting to play tricks on me." He padded back to bed and fell asleep.

Chapter 46

———

JOE PULLED OUT HIS CELL and punched the code he had stored for Elizabeth. When he heard her pick up, he whispered, "Stitch, I'm in the attic over Falcon's garage. Both he and his wife are in the house. Please drive over here right away to mailbox 8236—I didn't raise the flag. I put some papers in there about ten minutes ago."

"What papers?"

"Records that will clear me. Text me when you have them. Also, call Detective Armstrong. Tell him the door leading out the back of the garage to the side yard is open. Now go."

"Joe—" The phone went dead.

Elizabeth dressed quickly and darted out to her car. It was still dark. Driving the speed limit, she swung into Turtle Grove Estates in less than fifteen minutes flat. She turned up Red Snapper Lane, jumped out of her car, opened 8236 and grabbed everything that was in the mailbox. She silently pulled away looking back at the Falcon garage. Everything was quiet. She stopped at the entrance to the development—called Detective Armstrong and sent a text message to Joe: "Mission accomplished." She closed her cell phone, drove home, and went back to bed—her eyes wide open, breathing fast, nerves on edge.

———

"BYE, LIZZY," HELEN YELLED. Elizabeth didn't hear her as she pushed her cart through the swinging doors and loaded her vehicle as fast as she could. She was way ahead of all the other carriers as she headed out of the yard. Twenty-two minutes later she was at her first mailbox. Like a robot, she opened the hatch, stuffed the mail, flipped the hatch shut and moved on. "Why didn't I think to ask him about his plan?" Pull. Stuff. Flip. "He and Armstrong set the time for the sting at nine o'clock. Only fifteen minutes." Pull. Stuff. Flip.

"Hi, Lizzy," Barbara called out waving as she jogged by. Elizabeth looked at her but didn't acknowledge the greeting. Her head hurt. Her stomach growled for more than the yogurt she ate before leaving the house—the second time. She had been rushing non-stop since she arrived at the post office. "I wish I could go to the Falcon's now. Then what? Knock and say, 'Oh, Mr. Falcon, I'm sorry to bother you, but I was wondering if Joe is here?'"

———

JOE KNEW ARMSTRONG heard his conversation with Elizabeth. He also knew Armstrong would be upset that he asked Elizabeth to get the documents, but he didn't care. After he held back confiding in her about the bullet, he wanted to demonstrate that he trusted her. Armstrong now had no choice but to go along with whatever Joe had in mind.

At exactly nine o'clock Joe crept to the edge of the attic stairs, slipped down two steps and sat on the narrow board. Teetering a bit, he kept most of his weight on his feet. Pulling the pistol from his pants pocket, he fired a shot into the attic roof.

The door from the kitchen to the garage banged opened. Falcon bolted through. He took a few steps to the workbench. Turned left. Turned right. Listening.

Mona called to him from the kitchen. "Walter, that sounded like a truck backfiring." She appeared in the doorway. "What are you doing in the garage?"

"Very smart, Mona, very smart. You're so stupid. That was a gunshot, and it sounded like it came from the garage."

"Hello, Walter. Mona, he's right, it was a gunshot. You see I wanted to get your attention. Do I have your attention, Walter?"

Falcon spun around and looked up. "You SOB. What are you doing in my garage?"

"Oh, now, Walter. I just wanted to ask you nicely to return my house to me, and, of course, there's the little matter of your framing me, and oh, yes, Linda's murder. That about covers it unless you have more confessions you'd like to make. What is it they say? Confessions are good for the soul."

"I'll get you good, Rocket."

"Oh, that's priceless, Walter. I've got the gun, but you're going to get me? Let's start with you and Linda."

"It was her idea, Rocket. She was a money-hungry cat. There was never enough for her. She came up with the scheme to embezzle the funds and to frame you."

"Yes, I saw that. I think everything is here in this box." Joe pulled the fake books from the attic floor onto his lap.

"How did you get that?" Walter said leaning against the fender of his Cadillac, inching closer to the dangling attic stairs to get a better look at the box Rocket was holding.

"Oh, Walter, you really should have changed the locks on my house, get that, Walter, *my* doors to *my* house! I waltzed right in, but I have to admit it took me some time to find this little treasure chest of goodies."

"That will be the first charge, Rocket—breaking and entering."

Ignoring Falcon's remark, Joe continued with his script. "Then, Walter, you made the mistake of killing Linda in your bed. Really, Walter, that wasn't very nice."

"That's a lie. I didn't kill her. You did."

"Well, I don't think the police will think it's a lie when they see the bullet I dug out of the box spring under the mattress, the mattress with a hole in it. You did replace the top bedding, but I'm sure with all the latest technology the police won't have any trouble finding her blood in the springs. Really, Walter, shooting her in your own bed. Tacky. Very tacky."

"Well, Mr. smarty-pants, the police will blame you. Linda threatened to blackmail you...to send you away for good this time, so you shot her."

"But, Walter I was up north, a good boy being shown the gate on my first hours of freedom. I'm good, Walter, but even I can't be in two places at one time. And then there is the matter of a duplicate blanket, matching the one on your couch that you wrapped Linda in and then shoving her body in the culvert just a day or two before the hurricane hit. You probably thought she was wedged so tightly she'd never come out. But then to drop the murder weapon into the canal, really Walter. I thought you were smarter than that."

Joe put the box up on the attic floor. He turned back to Falcon and took another step—now a third of the way down the ladder. "You made another mistake, Walter. You didn't think I would look in the Maine house. The papers in this box showed Linda's part in the plot, but the records in the Maine house will prove that you were the one who masterminded the scheme. Really, Walter, how stupid can you be. Did you keep the papers so you could gloat, so you could keep patting yourself on the back at how smart you were, how you conned me out of a year and a half of my life, and *my* house, not to mention all of *my* money? Were you going to frame me for Linda's murder, too?"

"You broke into my house...maybe you had somebody else kill Linda. You probably bought off Smitty. That's it isn't it, Joe? You paid Smitty to kill Linda. Well, it won't work, Joe. You see I didn't kill Linda."

Joe saw Mona silently float up behind Falcon. She was pointing a gun at his back.

"That's right, Joe, Walter didn't kill Linda. I did."

Walter twirled around to face his wife.

"Mona—"

"You bastard, Walter. How much dirt did you think you could throw at me? Well, no more. You see, I sent Linda, your lover, an email from your account letting her know that your stupid wife had returned to Maine early, and to come over. I wrote that you'd meet her in bed with a little champagne cocktail. You're so fond of champagne, Walter. I was hiding when she arrived. She undressed and laid on the bed, naked, except for some gold heels, waiting for you. You should have seen her face, Walter, when I came through the bedroom door with a gun in my hand. I walked right up to her and shot her in her evil little heart."

"But, Mona, you couldn't have...you couldn't have carried her to the canal."

"Oh, I had help."

"I knew Joe was responsible."

"No. Not Joe. Timothy.

"Timothy?"

"Oh, yes. He and I had drinks a while back, and we got to talking about our lives. I told him how you were cheating on me all the time and he said how much he wished he could get his hands on his sister's money. So we kept talking and talking until we came up with the perfect solution for both of us. All we had to do was wait for the opportunity."

"Was Timothy in the house, too? You can blame him, Mona. You'll get off."

"No, he wasn't in the house. I called him to let him know that Linda was dead and to hurry over. He and I wrapped her in the blanket, took all the bedding and put it in his car, then remade the bed. We waited until just before midnight and together shoved her body in the pipe."

"Mona, I love you—"

"Oh, please, Walter, enough of your lies. Now it's your turn, Walter."

Mona stepped closer to her husband. Walter's face contorted. His hands grabbed his chest. "My heart. Mona. Mona. Get my nitro...my nitro, Mona." Falcon fell to his knees, face contorted in pain, eyes pleading...then slumped to the floor. Armstrong and two officers charged into the garage just as a second shot rang out.

Joe looked from Falcon to Mona lying on the floor.

"Goodbye, Walter," Mona whispered. The gun slipped from her limp fingers as she sprawled on the floor, blood draining from her lifeless body.

Chapter 47

——

JOE DIDN'T MOVE. He remained perched on the attic stairs staring in disbelief. The scene had played out like a Greek tragedy before his eyes. An eerie calm filled the hot, humid air in the dim light of the garage.

Armstrong called the morgue on his cell phone. He told Sam he had two bodies that needed to be picked up in Turtle Grove Estates and gave him the address. Armstrong looked up at Joe who seemed frozen on the steps of the ladder.

Pocketing the gun, Joe slowly descended the stairs never turning his back on the carnage below. He stepped around Falcon's body and pressed the garage door button.

Inch by inch bright sunlight filled the garage. Joe blinked at the sight of Elizabeth's image pacing back and forth beside her truck parked in front of box 8236, her head down listening to the sounds emanating from the wafer in his pocket. To Joe, she looked like a beautiful strawberry sundae, red shorts, lemon sprinkles on her sandals, and a blueberry T-shirt stenciled with race cars and Daytona 500 in gold letters. Her cap lay on the street beside the mail truck, freeing her soft red curls to circle her face.

Feeling his eyes on her, Elizabeth stopped in her tracks, turned around and looked at the open garage. Her face lit up, raspberry-red lips parting into a wide smile.

Joe walked over to her, picked her up and swung her around in his arms. "We did it, Stitch. We did it!"

Armstrong had walked up to the mail truck. He cleared his throat. "Might I have a word with you two?"

Joe put Elizabeth down on her feet. She straightened her T-shirt and smoothed down her shorts. "Of course, Detective. That was some piece of work my client did in there, wasn't it?"

"Yes, Elizabeth, it was some piece of work."

"Did you find Smitty in the bushes," Joe asked.

"Yes, we did. Not a happy fellow. We heard him try to grab you, Joe. But I thought I heard another voice, definitely not yours. Who was that?"

"I don't know...but you heard Smitty?"

"Loud and clear and all on tape. In fact, the whole sequence of events is going to make for some mighty fine listening. Now, about those papers in the mailbox—"

"Oh, I have them, Detective. Picked them up shortly after Joe called me."

"Yes, we heard that conversation." A frown formed on Armstrong's face. "I might have thought you would ask me to secure those documents, Joe."

"I'm sure you understand that my client will want to confer with his lawyer about how to proceed to exonerate himself completely from the embezzlement charges and, of course, to receive restitution for the year and a half he was wrongly incarcerated, and there's the little matter of his house—"

"His lawyer. Yes, I see. Joe, I'll need your statement plus I have many questions. You, too, Elizabeth."

"What about Timothy?" Elizabeth asked.

"As soon as I heard Mona say he was involved I sent two officers over to his house to pick him up for questioning. I'm sure he'll be bound over for arraignment. That was a shocker."

"Not as much of a shock as hearing Mona say she killed Linda," Joe said.

"That's for sure." Armstrong looked over at the garage. "Here comes Sam to pick up the Falcons and I see my boys have finished with the yellow tape. Quite a crime scene. Joe, can I talk to you this afternoon at the department with your lawyer, of course?"

"Certainly, after I check with him. Around two okay?"

"Fine. And Elizabeth, tomorrow morning?"

"Before work. Seven?"

Armstrong nodded in agreement. "Miss Stitchway, Private Investigator, I look forward to working with you in the future."

"Thanks, Detective Armstrong. That sounds great to me."

Armstrong pushed his glasses up on his nose, smiled, and turned to meet with Sam who had backed the wagon into the Falcon driveway.

Joe clasped her hand and kissed her smooth, soft knuckles. "How about giving me a lift to my Harley?"

"Where is it?"

"Chained to the rack at the clubhouse."

"Hop in. We'll finish my deliveries on Red Snapper Lane, and then I'll drop you off."

Elizabeth walked around to the driver's side of her truck and climbed in. Joe was already seated holding the last tray of mail in his lap. Elizabeth smiled over at him, released the brake, and slowly drove to the next mailbox.

Pull. Stuff. Flip.

Pull. Stuff. Flip.

Pull. Stuff. Flip...*kiss!*

The End

REVIEW REQUEST

Dear reader, I hope you enjoyed meeting a new friend, Elizabeth Stitchway. If you have the time, it would mean a lot to me if you wrote a review, your honest appraisal. What did you like most? Go to Amazon. Log in. Search: Mary Jane Forbes The Mailbox. Thank you!

ADD ME TO YOUR MAILING LIST

Please shoot me an email to be added to my mailing list for future book launches: MaryJane@MaryJaneForbes.com

Acknowledgements

Thanks to Roger and Pat Grady for their scrutiny of the first draft. Their efforts made for a much better story.

As ever, thanks to the NSERB (North Side Editorial Review Board)—Vera, Lorna, and Adele, for struggling through the initial draft, as well as my daughter Molly. It never ceases to amaze me how she comes up with salient, constructive criticism while tending to a husband and five children.

The Author

THE MAILBOX is Mary Jane's fifth novel and the book where she introduces her new sleuth, Elizabeth Stitchway.

Mary Jane has hinted that some time in the not too distant future, Elizabeth might meet Catherine Hainsworth, Hutch Hutchinson, and Daytona Pete her friends from the *House of Beads Mystery Series.*

Stay tuned at:
MaryJaneForbes.com

BOOKS BY MARY JANE FORBES
FICTION

<u>Inheritance Trilogy</u>
Contested, Torn, Lockdown,
Heist, Broken, Moment

<u>Gifts of Love Trilogy</u>
A Toy for Christmas, A Ghostly Affair
Love is in the Air

<u>*Bradley Farm Series*</u>
Bradley Farm, Sadie, Finn
Jeli, Marshall, Georgie

<u>*The Baker Girl*</u>
One Summer, *Promises,*
A Cupcake to Die For

<u>*Twists of Fate Series*</u>
The Fisherman, a love story
The Witness, living a lie
Twists of Fate, daring to dream

<u>*Murder by Design, Series:*</u>
Murder by Design
Labeled in Seattle
Choices, And the Courage to Risk

<u>*Elizabeth Stitchway, PI, Series*</u>
The Mailbox, Black Magic,
The Painter, Twister

<u>*House of Beads Mystery Series*</u>
Murder in the House of Beads
Intercept, Checkmate
Identity Theft

Novels – standalone
The Baby Quilt, The Message...Call Me!

Short Stories
Once Upon a Christmas Eve, a Romantic Fairy Tale
The Christmas Angel and the Magic Holiday Tree

Visit: www.MaryJaneForbes.com

Made in the USA
Monee, IL
13 June 2023

35739495R00115